More Cherry Harvest Stories: Sophie, Shayna, and Sarah

More Cherry Harvest Stories: Sophie, Shayna, and Sarah

Amy Wachspress

Woza Books
Books that Raise the Spirits

Woza Books
Oregon City, Oregon
(707) 468-4118
www.wozabooks.com

Cover design: Anjelica Colliard
Cover photo: Akili Reed Wachspress
Book design: Amy Wachspress

Publisher's Cataloging-in-Publication Data

Wachspress, Amy
  More Cherry Harvest Stories: Sophie, Shayna, and Sarah / by Amy Wachspress – 1st ed. – Oregon City, Oregon : Woza Books, 2026

ISBN: 978-0-9788350-7-1

Summary: This volume includes three character backstories (now novellas) not included in the original novel *Memories from Cherry Harvest*, a multigenerational family saga painted on the broad canvas of nations at war and in peace that explores the physics of memory, the survival of trauma, and the interconnected relationships between physical and spiritual reality.

1. FIC044000 FICTION / Women. 2. FIC045000 FICTION / Family Life / General.
3. FIC018000 FICTION / LGBTQ+ / Lesbian.

Library of Congress Control Number: 2025916961

Printed in the United States of America
10 9 8 7 6 5 4 3 2 1

About the "Deleted Scenes"

This volume is intended for people who enjoyed *Memories from Cherry Harvest* and would like to read more from the *Cherry Harvest* world. The editorial staff involved with publication of the book asked me to remove the sections about Sophie, Shayna, and Sarah because they believed these sections were not as compelling as the rest of the book, they slowed the pace, and they made the book too long. Perhaps those editors were correct. Perhaps not. But I didn't want the book to become a slog that would prevent people from finishing it. Furthermore, I had to agree to cut those scenes in order to have the book published at all. I could have self-published it, but I wanted to have the book published by an established publishing company and this was my chance. Back at that time, self-publishing was not as easy as it is now.

I put heart into the Sophie, Shayna, and Sarah sections over many years and was sad to excise them from the book in order to get it published. I have re-edited them and in *More Cherry Harvest Stories* I make them available to readers who might wish to delve into them. If you are one of those readers, I thank you for supporting and appreciating me as a creative.

These three sections, which I think of as the "deleted scenes," last appeared in a 2009 version of the book. Originally they followed the Rina section. To remove these sections, I had to identify all the material in them that moved the plot forward, contributed to the development of the characters and their relationships with one another, and was necessary for the full presentation of the themes and constructs central to the book. I then found ways to move the essential material from these sections into other parts of the book in some fashion. Many things that I would have loved to retain were unfortunately not transferable.

The novel underwent many revisions and transformations after these sections were removed. I revised the book to follow a clear family line from Ruth to Rina to Miriam. To facilitate this change, I made Sophie barren. I was reluctant to do away with her sons and the dimension of her as a mother, and I had misgivings about abandoning the exploration of the complexity of her relationship with her husband, but I couldn't see any way to retain that material in the new version. You will find her original backstory in the Sophie section included in this volume, which diverges from the storyline found in the final version of *Memories from Cherry Harvest* as published.

In 2009, before the extensive work that I did on the book to prepare it for publication, and before the removal of the Sophie, Shayna, and Sarah sections, the rocky relationship between Ruth and Rina was never fully resolved. Their original failure to reconcile appears peripherally in the Sophie and Sarah sections of *More Cherry Harvest Stories*. I think *Memories from Cherry Harvest* reads better and is more satisfying as it is in final form, with the reconciliation between mother and daughter.

I had the hardest time of all removing Sarah's section. There are so many aspects to her story that I didn't want to lose from the book. I was surprised that the editors insisted the book would be better without it. I sometimes wonder if those editors had a problem with Sarah's sexual orientation as a queer woman. I will never know. I'm especially pleased to finally put Sarah's coming-of-age story out into the world in this book of extended scenes.

I hope that you, Dear Reader, find something of value to take along with you into your life from my words after you have read *More Cherry Harvest Stories*.

Amy Wachspress
September, 2025

SOPHIE

I never made a conscious choice to attend college. I went because my parents expected it. I didn't know what I wanted to study, but that probably didn't matter. I think my father sent me to college to find a college-educated husband who would be a good provider. Once I was there, however, I enjoyed it. My classes were interesting enough. I was organized and applied myself to my studies; but I was more interested in my social life than my education. I was stylish, attractive, and (dare I say it) fun, so there was never a shortage of young men knocking on my door. Throughout my freshman year, I made a point of dating several men at once so none of them would become too possessive. I wasn't ready to compromise my freedom by getting too serious about any one man. I enjoyed flirtation.

My reticent younger sister, Irina, who visited me surprisingly often, could not comprehend my indifference toward my studies since she was desperate to leave home and attend college.

"The whole point of a college education is wasted on you," Irina scolded, in exasperation, as she tossed her backpack on my bed and her sleeping bag on the floor of my dorm room on one cold, gray Friday in February. "For a few years you have the opportunity to focus entirely on your studies, without the pressure of outside worries."

I had heard this before and was inclined to ignore her. "How can you travel so light?"

"It's just a weekend. How many things can a person wear in two days?"

"Tons. I couldn't even fit two days' worth of shoes in that thing." Then, glancing at Irina's hiking boots, I asked, "Did you roll a G.I. for his footwear?"

"Shut up!" she replied, with a good-natured laugh. "I have a present for you; but if you keep insulting me then I'll keep it for myself." Irina opened the backpack and removed a garment wrapped in lavender tissue paper, which she handed to me. I folded back the tissue paper to find a slinky, satin, black undershirt with delicate lacework trim. "The moment I saw it, I knew I had to get it for you. The woman in the store called it a teddy."

"The workmanship in the lace is exquisite. This must have been expensive."

"Not at all. I got it at a thrift shop. I think it's an antique or a Victorian replica. Try it on," Irina urged, pleased with my reaction.

I removed my blouse and slipped the teddy over my head. It fit perfectly. As I gazed at my image in the mirror, I felt a sense of déjà vu.

"You look sort of different," Irina commented uncertainly. We both stared at my reflection in the mirror, transfixed. Then I hastily removed the teddy and meticulously folded it back into the tissue paper.

"There's something special about it, isn't there?" Irina asked.

"There is."

Later, as I lay in bed listening to Irina's even breathing as she slept on the floor next to me, I thought about the teddy. I imagined I could hear it whispering to me from the drawer.

As soon as my sister left on Sunday, I put the teddy on and stared into the mirror. As if in a trance, I found some bobby pins and put my hair up. Looking at my reflection again, I felt as though I needed to remember something. I sat on the edge of my bed, closed my eyes, and waited, even though I had no idea what I was waiting for. Slowly, images floated into my mind. I saw myself in a white lacy dress, buttoned up the front over the contours of my corseted hourglass figure. I held a ruffled parasol and walked in a spring garden. I was a Victorian woman. A rose appeared, and then an entire basket of brilliant red roses. I could smell their intoxicating fragrance. Then the images and sensations faded.

That was the first time.

The teddy launched me on a fascination with Victorian culture. I checked books out of the library and pored over pictures of nineteenth-century wallpaper, furniture, dresses, shoes, and hats. I took a course in Victorian and Edwardian history and another in Victorian literature. I read some of Elizabeth Barrett Browning's poems so often that I memorized them. I spent hours combing antique shops, yard sales, and flea markets for "relics" (as I referred to my finds). I was reclaiming a culture that had belonged to me once upon a time, somewhere. The more I learned about the Victorians, the more Victorian images came to me when I sat quietly and cleared my mind of extraneous thoughts. At some point, I realized I was remembering, not imagining, and I felt certain I had lived a previous life during the Victorian Era.

In my sophomore year, I declared my major in history. I had pledged a sorority the previous year and when I returned in the fall, I moved into the sorority house, where I happily gossiped and swapped clothing, shoes, and accessories with my sorority sisters. I continued to date several young men at once, keeping them at arm's length, even though most of them would have liked to move in closer than the length of my arm.

"How do you know when you meet the right person?" I asked Mama.

"It's different for different people. For me, with your father, it dawned on me slowly that I could make a life with him."

When I met Max, the thought of a life together did not slowly dawn on me; it fell on me like a piano. After I told Papa that I had "met my match," he refashioned my words into "Sophie has met her Max."

Max and I had known each other only a few months before we became engaged. It seemed obvious to both of us that we were meant for each other. Max was a senior and he planned to go to medical school. I wanted to finish my undergraduate degree before marrying him. We shared the belief that sex was best saved for marriage and we settled in for a long engagement. My parents hosted a formal engagement party for us as soon as school ended for the summer. They wanted to show off the budding doctor I had snagged. Max's parents drove down from Buffalo with Max's younger sister for the party. Much to my parents' delight, Max's parents played bridge. The foursome spent many hours becoming acquainted over the card table.

That summer, I worked in Aunt Malka's deli, while Max landed a summer job in a pharmacy, where he learned a great deal of useful information about prescription drugs. We didn't see each other as often as we would have liked; but Max had been accepted to medical school and we would be living near each other when school started again, so we were patient. We had our whole lives together ahead of us.

On the first day of my return to college to begin my junior year, Max took me out to eat. It was a humid evening, with summer still beating its hot wings in the thick air. I watched from my upstairs window as Max parked his car and walked up the path to the door of the sorority house. He wore white linen trousers and a white polo shirt. He looked like a doctor already, immaculate and self-assured, someone you could trust with your life. A couple of yards from the door, he glanced up and noticed me at the open window framed by white lace curtains. We smiled as our eyes met and I raised a hand in greeting.

In that instant of recognition, my blood ran cold. Something deeply and disturbingly familiar registered in the back of my mind when I saw Max's bemused, rather paternalistic, expression. Something long-buried reared its head and peered through the mist into my consciousness, and for a brief inexplicable moment my heart raced. Then I heard my name shouted from the bottom of the stairs by one of my sorority sisters and I snapped back to the summer's day and the evening with Max that stretched ahead of me like a carpet rolled out to greet me. I took one last glance in the mirror and patted my hair. I went to him.

A few weeks later, I visited Irina, who had left home that fall and begun art school. She had swiftly distanced herself from the family and I didn't like it. I had decided to make an effort to spend more time with her. As I sat on Irina's bed in her dorm, I asked, "Have you ever met someone and had the feeling that you knew them before?"

Irina pulled a sweater over her tousled hair. "What do you mean?"

"Have you ever met someone and it seemed right off the bat as if he was more than familiar and that you already knew him, without needing to get to know him?"

"This is about Max, isn't it? You've got it bad."

"It is about Max, but it could be about anyone. I mean that feeling of having known someone already the minute you meet him."

"How would you have known him already?"

"Like in a previous life," I mumbled. "Never mind. I must sound crazy."

"You sound like you're in love. I hope it happens to me some day."

I appreciated the fact that she was taking me seriously and so I continued. "I'm not explaining this very well. It's not just about Max or even about people, as a matter of fact. I get this feeling of recognition with objects too. I sometimes pick up something and feel like I held it before, a long time ago, in a different life. Have you ever seen a picture in a book of a different place and time and recognized it?"

"Yes."

Our eyes locked. She knew exactly what I was describing. She knew it firsthand.

She hesitated before she continued, "Sometimes I see a pattern on an object. Usually an African object or an object created by indigenous people, like Native Americans. An object of art or everyday use, like a basket or a blanket. And I recognize the pattern. I realize that I know variations of the pattern. It's an abstract kind of thing. I see in my mind's eye different versions of the same pattern."

"Do you imagine the pattern or the object, or do you remember it?"

"It's more memory than imagination," Irina answered hesitantly, almost reluctantly. "I remember different versions. Then I draw them or adapt them in my work. I have no idea how I could remember these things or where I saw them before."

"It happens to me too, just as you described. I believe I can remember things that happened in a previous life. I'm not learning something fresh but rather remembering it. For me it happens with Victorian and Edwardian objects, especially clothing but also, like you said, objects of everyday use. And it happens sometimes with Max."

"What do you mean with Max?"

"I think I knew him in a previous life."

"You're serious."

"I am." If I could accept her description of her experience then I expected her to accept my description of mine.

"It happens to me primarily with the patterns I see on tribal and indigenous art. I've never felt as though I was recognizing a person."

"Never with people?"

"Not so far."

I married Max in August, after I graduated from college. Wrapped in a fantasy of pearls and lace, I walked down the aisle on my father's arm. My parents threw a huge wedding and invited everyone, including people I had never met. My mother and I spent that entire summer planning the wedding. We were in our element making all the arrangements. Although we didn't realize it as it happened, my wedding was the last time our family came together in the good ways that we could be together. Irina, who went by the name Rina now, spent very little time with the family. Sarah left for college two weeks after the wedding, and when she came home to visit she was preoccupied and aloof. I became busy with my new husband and the community service work that I did through the temple; so it took me quite a while to realize the distance that had grown between me and my sisters.

The year after we married, I became pregnant. I would not be lying if I said that neither Max nor I was more excited about the pregnancy than Papa. He came up with an excuse to stop by our house every day to admire my growing belly. One morning he came ostensibly to bring me the newspaper!

"Papa, we have the paper delivered."

"Well here's another one. Did you eat a good breakfast?"

"I just woke up, I haven't eaten anything yet."

"I'll make you scrambled eggs. Protein builds a strong baby. He's going to be a baseball player."

"How are you so sure it's a boy?"

"Because it's my turn to have a boy."

"Go to work, Papa. I'll scramble some eggs and eat them."

So it went. Papa bought stuffed animals, wooden trains, a rattle, and a sterling silver spoon for his forthcoming grandchild. As my due date approached, he produced larger objects, such as a crib, high chair, and dresser.

"I warned you. This is how he is with babies," Mama reminded me. "You don't remember, of course; but your father adores his babies. He would have had a yard full of them if I had agreed to it."

When I went into labor, just before dawn on a rainy October morning, I asked Max not to call my parents until after the baby arrived. I didn't want my father pacing the waiting room for hours like a cartoon character. Max had chosen to specialize in obstetrics for his medical degree; but when it came to the birth of his own baby, he could not focus on the medical aspects and instead hopped exuberantly around the delivery room like a lunatic heron.

I had an easy labor and delivery, and by early afternoon had given birth to a healthy boy with rosy skin and strong lungs, which he exercised the moment he emerged. Elated, Max and I were ready to share our joy so I called Papa at work. I was still on the phone with Mama when he materialized in my hospital room. Mama laughed at the news of Papa's instant appearance on the scene and hung up so she could join us.

Papa's doctor had recently persuaded him to give up cigars, so he had purchased a box of bubblegum cigars, which he distributed grandly to everyone in his path from the moment I informed him of the arrival of his grandson.

We named our boy Samuel, after Max's grandfather; but Papa called the baby Shmulek (the Yiddish version of Samuel). It was a delight to see Papa so gleeful. My father was a decent man, a generous man, and he deserved this happiness, which confirmed my faith that justice prevailed in the mysterious scheme of the universe. I never felt more like a good daughter.

Sammy was a happy and self-contained baby, who giggled and gurgled contentedly. He rarely cried unless hungry. With so much help from my doting parents, I fared well as a first-time mom. When I was worn out, I called my mother, who usually dropped everything and came over to take the baby to give me a break. One or the other (or both) of my parents stopped in to see Sammy almost every day. Max asked me if it bothered me to have my parents around so much. It truly did not. I loved it.

After completing his internship, Max progressed to his residency in obstetrics and gynecology. He was an intensity addict, who loved doctoring families through that powerfully magical time surrounding the birth of a child. He gave his patients his undivided attention, energetically sharing in their excitement and expectation; and he went the extra mile to help families cope if the going got rough so they had every chance of enjoying their new baby when it arrived. He had a sign in his office that read "NO BIRTH IS ROUTINE."

I was a bit jealous of Max, with his solid profession and a wide open future. Even though I shared in that wide open future, I wondered what profession would be right for me eventually. In the meantime, there was Sammy and I felt content. I organized a play group with other mothers of babies from our temple and we met twice a week, usually at my house. In those early years, it seemed as though everything Max and I touched turned to gold. Sammy was adorable and duly adored. Aunt Ida spent almost as much time fawning over Sammy as Mama, who said her grandson was the most over-stimulated baby in the county. He was showered in toys, books, clothing, and attention; and he thrived on it. As he grew into a toddler, he investigated every single toy, looked at every page of every book, wore every piece of clothing, and laughed and smiled at everyone he encountered.

Sarah, who had become guarded and reserved after she went away to college, began calling me every couple of weeks after Sammy was born to hear about everything he did. I welcomed her phone calls as an opportunity to leave the door open if she should decide to talk about her own life, but she never did.

Rina (as she insisted on being called) remained even more reticent than Sarah. She kept her distance, never phoning our parents. I thought she would spend more time with the family after I had Sammy, but she showed no interest in Sammy. Apparently she had bigger fish to fry. She was busy launching a career as a graphic artist and could not be pried out of her intellectual and cultural circle in New York. Little me at home with my baby in the suburbs bored her.

The baby brought me and Max closer in our relationship. Max delighted in sharing his amazing birth stories from work with me and I never tired of hearing about the myriad miraculous ways babies entered the world. My sexual appetite increased because making love to the father of my baby aroused me, and Max certainly did not protest when I put my hands on him more often at night.

When I wasn't busy admiring my remarkable, entertaining son or making love to my gifted, popular husband, I was busy maintaining my immaculately spotless house. I had a charmed life and was grateful for it. When Sammy grew into a sturdy and mischievous toddler, I took up cooking with a vengeance, preparing elaborate gourmet meals. I had read in a child development book that a toddler's world was his laboratory in which he experimented. So I put Sammy in the figurative laboratory, which was physically under the kitchen table, with kitchen equipment (pots, spoons, plastic storage containers), or paper and crayons, or toys. Sammy experimented in the laboratory while I studiously sautéed, chopped, marinated, rolled, sprinkled, ground, baked, sizzled, steamed, and roasted.

My contentment was disrupted when the clear surface of the undisturbed pond of my existence was abruptly broken by Rina. I never did get the whole story from Mama; but the gist of it was that Rina announced she was moving in with her lover, Arthur, and Papa disowned her on the spot, not because Rina was living in sin, not even because Arthur wasn't Jewish, but primarily because Arthur was, as Papa said, a "*schvartze.*" In Yiddish, the word literally meant "black," but it was used as a derogatory term for Blacks, as in "don't ever ever ever marry one." I didn't know if I was more upset by my parents' prejudice or Rina's lack of concern for their feelings. I scolded Rina for being so confrontational. If she had handled the situation gracefully, then perhaps our parents would have accepted the situation. Rina said it was not a situation, it was her life, and she didn't care if they accepted it or not. "Nate has wanted to wash his hands of me for years. Now he can," Rina declared. I was angry at the whole lot of them, including Sarah, the family icy Switzerland, who assiduously refused to get involved in the conflict.

The rift between Rina and our parents unbalanced me. I felt like a child of divorce. It disturbed me to have our family in such disorder. I talked about it incessantly with Max, who listened graciously without attempting to offer advice. My parents behaved as if Rina had died and she showed no interest in reconciling with them. I developed my own coping mechanism to escape from our family strife by going "junking." I visited flea markets, garage sales, and estate sales. I crammed knickknacks into every corner of my house. Pin dishes. Pitchers. Doilies. Candlestick holders. Vases. Ceramics. Crystal. I found serenity in these beautiful objects from the past, which were like old friends lost and then rediscovered, a cycle completed. Their beauty and the order I gave to these objects in my home filled my need to set things right.

In the spring, I invited Rina, Arthur, and Sarah to stay with us for a weekend. I wanted to offer Arthur some semblance of a welcome to the family. I warned my father in advance. "Papa, I called to let you know that Rina and Arthur will be spending the weekend. I didn't want you to pop in unannounced and be taken by surprise."

"I don't know any Rina," he replied sharply, and hung up. I didn't hear from him for a week afterward.

The weekend went well. Max's genuine warmth put Arthur at ease. They shared a passion for jazz and delved into Max's record collection while we sisters chatted in the kitchen with Sammy toddling between us. Sarah and Rina helped me start flower seeds in my new little greenhouse in the back yard. Sarah showed Sammy how to push the big sunflower seeds down into the dark earth with his dimpled finger. Max and Arthur went to the hardware store and brought home a hammock, which they slung between two elm trees in the back yard. They took pictures of each other playing with Sammy in the hammock. In the evening Sarah fell asleep rocking gently in it. I didn't want to let my sisters go at the end of the weekend. Seeing Rina so comfortable and happy with Arthur relieved some of my anxiety. I hoped that one day my parents would accept my sister's choices.

During the year that followed, we sisters didn't see much of one another, although we spoke more often by phone after the successful weekend visit. A couple of times, Max and I met Rina and Arthur in the city for dinner. Rina was receiving more work offers than she could accept. She and Arthur had landed a substantial job together illustrating children's books. I inferred that they were making good money.

Meanwhile Sarah was in her last year at Vassar and planned to go on for a teaching credential. She had become quite the career woman. Sometimes I envied her; but I was enjoying being a mommy too much to think about going to work. Max and I decided to have another baby, which would further delay any career plans for me. While we looked forward to having another child, we agreed we didn't want more than two children, which seemed to us like just the right number.

When I called Rina to tell her I was pregnant, she replied, "I have some news too."

I could hardly believe it. Both of us at the same time! "Do you want Max to deliver?"

"No thanks. Arthur's cousin is a homebirth midwife and she practices here in the city. We're fine."

"Is that safe? Don't you have a doctor?"

"We're fine," she repeated more firmly. I detected that annoyingly condescending tone in Rina's voice that meant she was trying to be patient while the rest of the world caught up with her maverick ideas. I tried to ignore it. I also chose not to express my disapproval that they were not married. I knew she would immediately clam up if I criticized her. Sadly, my new niece or nephew would be born out of wedlock and would be forced, needlessly, to deal with the consequences of that. Rina could be so selfish.

After we hung up, it dawned on me that Mama and Papa would remain ignorant of Rina's news unless I told them. I agonized over it and wondered if this might prompt them to make an overture of reconciliation. I had to tell them, but how?

I called Sarah. "Have you spoken to Rina?" I asked tentatively.

"About the baby? Yup. It's wonderful both of you at once!"

"We have to tell Papa and Mama."

"It won't make any difference."

"Of course it will. They might give up this feud because of it."

"I wouldn't hold my breath."

I mentioned it as casually as possible to Mama while we walked to the park with Sammy. She thanked me for the information and changed the subject. It was a shocking brush-off. I wondered if she would tell my father, but didn't have the courage to ask.

A couple of months before my baby was due, Rina called me at eleven o'clock on a Sunday morning and greeted me with, "She's here, Auntie Soph."

"It's a girl?"

"It's a girl. Labor is one wild ride! You should have warned me," Rina exclaimed in a voice vibrating with the birthing day euphoria I remembered so well.

"You can't really warn someone sufficiently, it's something you have to experience." I heard music and laughter in the background. "It sounds like a party there."

"A lot of people are here."

"Where are you?"

"At home. She was born about an hour ago."

"So you had her at home and everything is OK?"

"Everything is great. We have three midwives here and a lot of friends. We're fine, absolutely fine. The baby is spectacular."

"What is her name?"

"That's an interesting story. We had a lovely African name picked out for her, but the moment I laid eyes on her, I thought she looked like a Miriam. Arthur agreed. So we named her

Miriam; you know, after that adopted sister of mother's who died in the war. I always remembered the story about her trying to rescue all those children and her bravery."

"Miriam," I repeated aloud, trying it out. "Listen, I'm on my way over."

"You don't have to race out," Rina said with a laugh. "We're not going anywhere."

"I wouldn't miss this for the world. I want to see my niece."

As soon as I put down the phone, I packed up Sammy to head into the city. I called Max with the news and warned him I might spend the night. When Max heard that Rina had given birth at home, he hit the roof. "That is the most dangerous, most irresponsible thing! What were they thinking?!"

"They're fine. She has a midwife. In fact she has three midwives over there." I didn't like his tone, even though in theory I agreed with him.

"I don't care if she had a hundred midwives. What if something had gone wrong?"

"It didn't."

"Three midwives does not equal a doctor or a fully equipped hospital."

"I think it was a brave thing to do," I said, defending Rina's choice. Only moments before, I had been of the same opinion as Max; but I didn't like him blasting my sister like that and so I took her side.

"Brave? To put a baby at risk? To risk one's own health and safety?"

"What's done is done and it turned out fine. I have to go." I hung up before the conversation could turn into a major argument.

I was suddenly furious with our family for being so critical of Rina. Why did everyone have to find fault with Rina's way of doing things? She was a visionary, a trailblazer. She refused to be muscled back into the dark ages by men stuck in backward thinking, like my bullying husband and father. I wished that I had taken a stronger stand in Rina's defense in the past. I was angry at Max and Papa. I was excited about the birth of my niece. I was pregnant, hormonal, and fuming. I drove to my parents' house, burst in the door like one of the Furies, and ordered Mama to get in the car.

"What's going on? What happened?"

"Your granddaughter happened, and we're going to see her. Get in the car."

Perhaps if I had not been so distraught, Mama would have managed to refuse to go with me, but I took her by surprise with my emotional outburst. On the drive into the city, Mama said little; mostly because she couldn't get a word in edgewise. Trapped in the car with me, she was forced to listen to my extended tirade on the complete idiocy of men. Sammy sat wide-eyed in his car seat clutching a stuffed dog until the motion of the car put him to sleep.

By the time we pulled up at Arthur and Rina's house, I had spent my wrath and found myself neck-deep in forcing a confrontation between my mother and sister after more than two years of non-communication. This may not have been the best time for it, since my sister had given birth to a baby only hours before. I told Mama, "I can't force you, but I think you should go in there."

"I'm not sure she would want me in there," Mama pointed out dubiously. "It might ruin one of the happiest days of her life. Why don't you go in first to see about it. I'll stay here with Sammy so you don't have to wake him just yet."

As I rang the bell, I panicked. What had I done?

When the door opened, I was swept up in what felt like Mardi Gras. The house was packed with jubilant celebrants. Paper storks hung from the lighting fixtures. The dining room table was laden with food. Music blasted. An eclectic mix of people of all different races and ages danced and drank champagne together. On the couch, propped up on mauve, purple, and burgundy pillows, Rina and her baby girl held court. I promptly burst into tears as Rina's guests parted like the Red Sea to let me through.

"My sister," Rina called to her friends. "This is Soph, my sister." Rina patted the couch next to her. "Come sit," she commanded. So I sat, wiped the tears from my cheeks, and took my niece Miriam in my arms.

"She's absolutely beautiful," I cooed. "She's perfect." Miriam had an abundance of softly curled hair that ringed her nut-brown face. I looked up from my amazing niece and blurted, "Oh Rina, I'm sorry, I wasn't thinking. Max was horrid about the home birth. I was angry and, well, it's a long story. The upshot is that I have Mama in the car."

"She's in the car? Here?"

I burst into slightly hysterical laughter. "Poor Mama, I ran into her house like a demon and ordered her into the car. But she wants very much to see the baby."

"Then what's she doing in the car?"

"She's watching Sammy. He fell asleep," I answered, as if this was the real reason she had waited in the car.

"Well you had better go fetch her." She patted my arm. "It will be OK."

"I'll be right back." I handed Miriam back to Rina.

"Find Arthur and warn him before you bring her in," Rina requested.

I found Arthur and congratulated him, gave him a hug, and informed him that I had brought Mama. Then I went back to the car, where I gathered my things, realizing that I certainly was not spending the night, and handed my handbag and diaper bag to Mama so I could hold Sammy, who was beginning to wake up.

Arthur held the heavy, beveled glass door open for us. In the entryway, he welcomed Mama with no particular discernible emotion and pointed to the living room. I was worried, until he held me back as Mama proceeded into the house and reassured me, "It's good you made her come. It's awkward, but it's a good thing."

I saw Mama bend stiffly to give Rina a hug and then Rina handed the newborn to her. I could not hear their quiet conversation. Mama peered into the baby's face and sat down on the couch next to Rina. Sammy was fully awake and hungry so I became preoccupied with getting him something to eat. While in the kitchen, I talked to a few of Rina's friends. When I returned to my mother and sister, they remained exactly as I had left them, except that the baby had disappeared. Mama sat with her hands folded neatly in her lap.

"Where's the baby?" I asked.

"Arthur's checking her diaper," Rina informed. "Sit with us." Rina pointed to a chair next to the couch. As I sat, I saw a crippled man with deformed legs playing peek-a-boo with Sammy. I remembered him from Rina's graduation. He was one of her fellow students at art school.

"Tell me all about the birth," I demanded.

Arthur brought Miriam back and I held her while Rina, glowing, recounted the details of

Miriam's birth. The baby gazed at my face with wide open, alert eyes.

The crippled man wheeled around the house chasing Sammy, who giggled, while guests dodged them. He was pretty fast for a man in a wheelchair. Soon Sammy's infectious laughter rose above the conversation and, as usual, he delighted everyone within range. His charisma always astounded and delighted me.

I figured Mama was probably feeling uncomfortable and would welcome a diplomatic departure whenever I was ready. Reluctantly I suggested, "Mama, we should probably head home. I have to fix dinner for Max; and Sammy is over-excited."

Rina laughed. "Can't Max fix his own dinner? And whatever will we do to entertain TJ if you take Sammy away from him?"

"I'll come back when the house isn't crowded," I promised. "Remember to take care of yourself. Tell these people to go when you need to sleep."

"It's OK. I'm good. Thanks for coming so quickly and for bringing Mother."

Rina took Mama's hand in hers and said, "Thank you for coming, Mother. It made the day complete." Mama kissed Rina on both cheeks. Rina continued, "She's your granddaughter. Don't be a stranger in our house because of the old bull." Tears of relief filled my eyes at her words. I hoped they would rebuild their relationship around this baby. But on the drive home my hope was shattered.

Mama drove because I was exhausted. I asked her what she thought about our visit.

"The truth?"

"Yes, certainly."

"Miriam is beautiful; however, I saw no sign whatsoever of our family's features in her face. Countless generations of Jews, thousands of years of tradition, thousands of years surviving oppression to retain our identity, ends in that house. And look at that house! I wonder how anyone can live amidst such disarray. Did you see those piles of magazines stacked against the dining room walls? Who needs to keep so many magazines? Those plants in saucers on the windowsills are leaving damp rings of mold. There weren't even curtains at the front windows. Any passerby can peer right in. Every surface in that house is piled with clutter and trash. Why bother to have tables or desks at all?

And her friends. The man in the wheelchair, poor fellow, seems normal enough, but what about those three godmothers? The fat godmother with the stringy graying hair obviously was not wearing a bra. Irina said she's a former teacher of hers. Did you see her kiss the Spanish woman? They're homosexuals. The swishy man in the ruffled apron who brought the trays of hors d'oeuvres around was also homosexual. That Oriental lover of his was so loud. I was embarrassed to watch them carry on the way they did. And how about the godmother who insisted on playing a saxophone solo for the baby? What kind of crazy person plays the saxophone for a newborn? That third godmother, Norma, I remember her name. She had such a stylish hat, but her make-up made her look like a raccoon. I have to wonder what kind of childhood awaits that baby. Can you imagine growing up in such chaos, surrounded by that bizarre assortment of misfits? And that child is neither fish nor fowl."

As I listened in astonishment as Mama described her perception of the scene we had just witnessed, I had to wonder for an instant if we had both been to the same house. I was shocked by her prejudices, and reminded that she came from another country and another era, and that she lived in an insular conservative Jewish community. Her world and Rina's world were light years apart.

"I don't approve, Sophie. I just don't. I can't force myself to approve. I'm extremely unhappy with her choices in life; but she's my daughter and, as God is my witness, I do want her to be happy. That is the truth. That was the one saving grace in today's visit; she appears to be happy. I am glad for that. God give me the strength for the rest of it."

"Are you angry with me for dragging you over there?"

"No, sweetheart, I'm glad I saw the baby. But please don't tell your father I went. You girls have moved on with your own lives. Your father is what I have left."

After Miriam's birth, Mama phoned Rina occasionally for news of her and the baby. Sometimes when Rina brought Miriam to my house, Mama would come to see her granddaughter, but she never went to Rina's house again.

I followed close on Rina's heels with my baby. When Joel arrived, I discovered how vastly different babies are from one another. Sammy had been an easy baby. Everything pleased him. He entertained himself. He slept well. He ate well. In contrast, Joel had colic for the first two months of his life and therefore had difficulty sleeping because his tummy hurt. I stumbled around in a haze of sleep deprivation. If I sat down for more than a few minutes, I nodded off. I frequently stretched out on the floor where Sammy could climb on me, chattering away, while Joel slept in snatches and I drifted in and out of consciousness.

Joel was an active and demanding baby who rapidly became a toddler with no attention span whatsoever. As a toddler, Sammy had been able to entertain himself for an hour with a set of plastic containers and a spoon. By contrast, Joel picked up one toy after another and discarded each one within seconds. He never stopped moving and became furious when restrained or unable to accomplish a physical task he had set for himself. He loved the outdoors and became cranky if we stayed inside all day. He could have lived at the park. He required my full attention during every waking hour. I was grateful for Sammy's imagination, which afforded me some measure of respite when he entertained Joel.

Papa saved my sanity. He never tired of reading the same story over and over again to Sammy or giving Joel pony rides around the living room on his back. Grandpa was their favorite toy, their favorite buddy, their favorite pet, their favorite partner in crime. Papa amazed me with the games he thought up and the activities he invented for his precious grandsons. No one held the attention of my whirling dervish Joel like Grandpa.

Right after I weaned Joel, I experienced a hormonal imbalance and Max diagnosed the cause as low estrogen. I was depressed for no particular reason. Max put me on the Pill, which improved my emotional state; however, I gained weight and felt sluggish. I still had mood swings and I suffered from insomnia. I realized that I wished I had a job to go to during the day instead of spending all my time at home with small children. I admired my father, who had served for many years as a city council member and was on the board of directors of our temple. What did I want to do when I grew up? Max would support me in going to graduate school, but I didn't know what I wanted to study.

When Sammy started kindergarten, I volunteered as the classroom mom, organizing parties and field trips for Sammy's class. I became the secretary of the PTA. I coordinated the school's annual fund-raising event. I attended the monthly school board meetings. I read *Robert's Rules of Order* and took a workshop at the community college in facilitating efficient meetings.

I invested a great deal of energy in maintaining a well-ordered house; which was challenging because my darling boys unraveled everything as quickly as I could neatly tie it up. I frequently resented Max's ability to waltz in and out as he pleased; his clothes "magically" laundered, his food "magically" cooked, and his house "magically" cleaned. I started to ask him to do things to help around the house. But why did I have to ask? Couldn't he see that the bathtub needed cleaning? Couldn't he do the dishes instead of assuming that I would do them? Why did I iron Max's shirts while he read the newspaper?

Early one Saturday morning, I woke from a deep sleep to find Joel eye-to-eye with me, demanding a bowl of cereal. As I rose from the bed in a stupor and reached for my robe, I noticed Max sitting up in bed next to me, reading, oblivious to Joel's needs. It had not occurred to him to intervene, to prevent Joel from waking me, to offer to get the child breakfast. I stopped dead in my tracks, removed my bathrobe, sat down on the bed, and said to Joel, "Daddy can get you cereal."

Max looked up from his book, befuddled. "Huh?"

"You are perfectly capable of getting a child cereal," I muttered.

"No, no I want Mommy to do it," Joel demanded in a dangerously shrill voice.

"What?" Max asked. "Does Joel want something?"

Joel teetered on the verge of a tantrum. I shrugged back into my bathrobe and waved an arm, dismissing Max. "Never mind." Max returned to his book.

Later that day, I overheard an acquaintance at temple complaining about how little her husband did around the house. I tuned right in to the conversation and soon found myself standing in a tight circle of women venting our frustrations. I had a few choice comments to contribute. One of the women, Anna, invited us to join a women's group she was starting. Anna was a professional therapist, but this group was a personal thing for her own benefit. The group would meet once a week. I had heard about women's groups but had never imagined joining one myself. I had a comical mental image of what went on at a women's group; yet when the real opportunity to share my concerns and frustrations with other women presented itself, I said, "Where do I sign?"

As I turned to leave the conversation, Anna tapped me on the arm and suggested, "I know it's none of my business, but have you told your husband how you feel about the housework? A lot of times, men just don't realize. They have to consciously change their behavior. Try talking to him about it."

The following Tuesday, I got up extra-early to go on a field trip with Sammy's kindergarten class. When we returned from the field trip, I took the boys for a routine check-up with the pediatrician and then went straight home to make dinner. After dinner, I had a PTA meeting. So I got the boys ready for bed and left them on the couch with Max reading stories while I ran out to the school. When I came home, exhausted, at nine o'clock, I found the house in a shambles. Not a dish had been washed, not a toy put away. The towels I had thrown in the washer during dinner sat in a damp lump at the bottom of the machine. Max, my handsome husband, sat in bed in his handsome pajamas reading a pristine medical journal.

"Would it be so difficult for you to clean up the kitchen? Or pick up after the children? Or do a load of laundry? I am not a live-in maid service!" I exploded, to Max's apparent bafflement, which infuriated me even more.

"I put the children to bed," he defended himself.

"After I bathed them, fed them, and sat them neatly on the couch in a row. I have other things to do with my life than clean up after three boys."

"Soph, be fair. I work at a highly demanding job to support you and the boys in the manner to which you are accustomed. I thought we had a partnership, a contract if you will, that while the boys are young, I work and your job is to maintain our home."

"Well you didn't read the fine print in the contract. The fine print says: Sophie is not a servant, she is entitled to have a life. Just because my activities earn no money doesn't mean they have no value."

"Of course your activities have value. I appreciate everything you do. You're a terrific mom and you manage the house like a well-run ship."

"A well-run ship? Can't you even think of an original metaphor?"

"Have I been remiss in showing my appreciation?" Max put on the wounded puppy look. It didn't work.

"Appreciation isn't the point. I shouldn't have to ask you for help. You should just do it. Do the dishes to give me a break. Iron your own shirts. If I have a meeting, like tonight, then you clean up after the boys, and you do the laundry. Don't assume that I am going to do everything.

I don't want to do everything. I have other interests. Other adult interests."

"I love you and I want you to be happy."

"Then do some house work." Why did I feel guilty making totally reasonable demands? Max made me feel irrational and humored.

On Sunday morning, Max went to the hospital before dawn to deliver a baby. He was just returning in the early afternoon as I was leaving to take the boys to a carnival at the park. We had fun and stayed later than I had intended. When we returned home, I discovered that Max had cleaned the house, done the laundry, ironed his shirts for the coming week, and was cooking dinner. He had set the dining room table with a tablecloth, candles, and wine glasses. He greeted me with a boyish smile and a kiss. Then he scooped the boys up and tickled them.

We ate a delicious meal of chicken, rice, and broccoli. Afterward, Max did the dishes while I put my feet up and read an article about making positive change in public schools that had been given to me by the principal at Sammy's school. Max gave the boys their bath and I read aloud to them and tucked them into bed with a kiss.

I came downstairs and sat next to Max on the couch. "Thank you. What a lovely evening."

"It makes such a difference?"

"The biggest difference." I wondered if he understood or if he just wanted to make me happy and didn't get why his help with the housework mattered. From that night on, Max made an effort to be more helpful and to share the burden of maintaining the household. Even so, he continued to annoy me with petty things that I tried not to mention. One moment I felt a rush of affection for him and the next moment utter exasperation at his insensitivity.

I did not want any more children, and fortunately Max had no quarrel with that. The last thing I needed was to start from scratch with another baby. Although he was a difficult toddler, Joel outgrew his fits of temper and frustration. He worshipped his big brother and, despite the fact that more often than not he obstinately refused to obey others, he usually obeyed Sammy's demands. Max joked that if Sammy told him to, Joel would fetch his brother's slippers and newspaper.

In the fall, when he began first grade, Sammy started playing soccer. Max coached the soccer team and I coached Max in my role as the "Team Mom."

I put Joel into a preschool for a year before he began kindergarten. We were both happy with this arrangement. He enjoyed playing with his little pals and boasting about what he did at "my school," as he called it. I systematically researched the career possibilities open to me, changing my mind weekly, often daily, about what I wanted to do with my life. And then my career found me, appearing out of nowhere from an unexpected quarter.

Sammy was bosom buddies with a Dominican boy whose family had fled an authoritarian regime in their homeland. Sammy and Salvador played at each other's homes frequently, so I became well-acquainted with the family. One day Sammy announced that Salvador was moving back to the Dominican Republic. I immediately called Sofia, Salvador's mother, who told me her husband had been taken by the Immigration and Naturalization Service (INS). He stood a good chance of being deported, which, she informed me tearfully, meant he would probably be tortured and killed. I had not known that the family was living in the United States illegally. Sofia and the children had not been detained, but the INS was aware of them. They were at risk of deportation as well.

Sofia hired an attorney named Alice, who specialized in immigration law. I had never heard of such a thing. I met Alice when I brought a casserole over to the family for dinner. I was immediately impressed with Alice's straightforward and compassionate style of working with the family.

I tried to help Sofia by organizing the soccer moms to take turns bringing food to the family in the evenings while Raoul was imprisoned. It came as a rude awakening to me when most of the other moms refused to have anything to do with the family anymore, even though they knew Sofia and her children well from sitting on the sidelines with them and cheering the boys on together at weekly soccer games.

I went to the house often and kept Sofia's children occupied so she could meet with Alice, who spoke with her softly in Spanish. One night, I asked Alice about the work that she did. A few weeks later, when Alice managed to obtain political asylum for the entire family, bringing Raoul home, I was hooked. On the night of Raoul's release I announced to Max that I intended to go to law school. Max slowly put his book down with a bemused expression.

"What's so funny?"

"Nothing."

"Yes something. What's so funny?" I nearly stamped my foot.

"It's just I don't know whether to take you seriously. What happened to becoming a chef, a dress designer, a writer, a museum curator, a school administrator, an anthropologist, and a textiles importer? How am I supposed to know when you've made a real decision? Now you want to be an attorney. That's fine. Attorney is fine."

"I would appreciate a less condescending tone. I'm an adult."

"You're an adult who changes her mind frequently on this subject. There's nothing wrong with changing your mind. I apologize if I insulted you."

"I'm serious."

"I wish you had come with an instruction manual, Soph. Honestly."

Sometimes I found myself blaming Max for the misdeeds of the entire male species, even though I knew that wasn't fair to him, but I couldn't help myself. "I'm going to look into law schools. You'll see, this one is for real."

"If you say so."

The following year, I really did start law school. I didn't try to take a full course load. Instead I arranged to matriculate more slowly than my younger classmates. Even so, adjusting to the new demands on my time posed a challenge. Max and I arrived at a pivotal moment in our relationship on the Wednesday that he ducked out when I had my women's group. At breakfast, Max announced he would not be home for dinner because he had to attend a department meeting at the hospital.

"Tonight is my women's group. The first Wednesday of the month. You know that. I expect you to watch the boys every first Wednesday," I reminded him, as I struggled to refrain from raising my voice.

"I have to go. It's my job."

"Well then go. But you need child care. Either find a babysitter or take the boys with you," I insisted stubbornly.

"Take the boys with me? To a department meeting?"

"Then find a babysitter."

"I don't have time to call around for a babysitter, Soph. Today is surgery. I have two hysterectomies and a tubal ligation to perform."

"The boys are your children too. Why do I have to ask you to watch the boys but you never have to ask me to watch them? You assume that I have them unless I make other arrangements. Stop assuming that if we're both busy, I'm the one who has to find a babysitter. How is it that you are never, never responsible for finding child care? Tonight I don't have them. You do. If you're busy then you find someone to take care of them. You make the arrangements."

"I told you. I'm in surgery today. I don't have time to find a babysitter."

"You're too busy yanking out women's ovaries to find a babysitter for your own children."

"Uterus. Just the uterus. We don't remove the ovaries. Don't be melodramatic. It's a medical procedure, nothing personal."

"Yank whatever you want to yank and make it as impersonal as you want to make it; but in between doing it, you find the time to arrange for a babysitter."

Max assumed his most authoritative, paternalistic, doctorly voice. "Sophie, we'll discuss this issue later. I'm sorry I disappointed you and I hope you can find a babysitter so you can go to your women's group." He turned cleanly on his heel and left for work.

Joel had appeared in the kitchen at the end of the argument. He stood crying in the doorway, his teddy bear dangling dejectedly from one little hand. I picked him up and set him on my lap and I cried with him in my frustration and rage.

When Max came home from his meeting that night, he found his bedroom door locked and the hide-a-bed in the guest room neatly made up for him. The next day he started running an ad in the newspaper for a live-in housekeeper and nanny. For once, he had a decent solution. "We are in the process of becoming a two-career household. We can afford this option for easing the burden on ourselves so let's do it," Max said. "You need time to study in the evenings and I'm often on call. Someone has to care for the boys. With a live-in, you can schedule your time for study and your time for family and never worry about child care."

He was essentially taking responsibility for child care so I forgave him and let him back into the bedroom. I wondered how other women, who weren't fortunate enough to be able to afford a live-in, managed. My heart went out to all the mothers, some of them who were on their own without a husband, who couldn't afford extra help and who worked full-time at a job. I hired a contractor to make modifications to the basement to turn it into a cozy, private apartment. We advertised in the newspaper for two weeks, interviewed eighteen people, and fell in love with Joyce, a Haitian. Joyce would live in the guest room until her apartment was completed. Hiring Joyce made such a huge difference for us that I wondered why we hadn't thought of it sooner.

Joyce elected not to share her full story with us. Something had happened that drove her from her homeland, something that kept her from having a family of her own. Whatever it was, she wouldn't talk about it. She was content to devote herself to our family. She adored our children and cared for them with abundant love and pride in all their accomplishments. The boys' affection for her quickly grew. I reinforced their relationship with her because it bought my freedom.

One time Rina asked me if it bothered me to have a servant raise my children.

"She's not a servant. She's one of the family. She lives with us as a member of the household. We provide her with room and board, the use of a car, and we pay her an excellent salary, much of which she is able to save."

"She saves her salary because she has no one and nothing to spend it on. She has no life of her own."

"What gives you the right to judge us, or her?" I asked hotly. "Ask her yourself whether or not she likes living with us, whether or not she's one of the family." Rina let the conversation drop. It seemed transparent to me that Rina's real problem was that Joyce was Black. It was Rina's issue, not mine, and I refused to shoulder it.

Joyce was one of the greatest gifts that came to me in this life. She brought harmony to my home. She took a lot of the stress off my marriage because I got along better with Max when I had time to pursue my own interests. I told her, often, how much I appreciated her.

One night, I took a break from my studies and proceeded to clean out my top dresser drawer. I sorted through my underwear and stockings, discarding items I no longer wore. At the bottom of the drawer I came across the teddy that Rina had given to me when I was in college. I never wore it, but I could never quite get rid of it either. In the past, whenever I put it on, it transported me.

I tentatively slipped the teddy on and gazed at my reflection. I slipped into a reverie as images poured into my consciousness. I was a Victorian lady sitting in a parlor, playing cards, wearing the teddy over a corset and under a peach-and-cream-colored dress with intricate lacework in the bodice. I wore a complicated hat and sat erect in a high-backed chair. Max came up behind me, glanced at my cards and placed a hand on my shoulder. He touched one of my cards with his finger. I didn't agree with his choice, but I played the card anyway. In this reverie, I feared my husband Max so I obeyed him. I knew he could physically hurt me, and that he had done so in the past. I felt trapped and couldn't breathe. I was confined in the corset, in the room, in the relationship.

In this trance-like state, a rush of understanding washed over me. Victorian-Sophie was married to Victorian-Max who abused her, bullied her, prevented her from becoming the woman she could have been. An awareness washed over me that in our present life together, we were working it out, finishing something started long ago. Trembling, I removed the teddy and placed it back in the bottom of my drawer. The images and the knowledge remained firm in my mind. Could I overcome this residual baggage and give Max a chance to get it right this time around? If I were to try to explain any of this to another living soul, they would have me committed. Except perhaps Rina, but we had not confided in one another about anything significant for a long time.

My Victorian memories would have to remain private. I began to secretly engage in the habit of sitting quietly and holding antique objects that I had collected, while inviting the images they brought into my mind; thus surfacing more and more of these former-life memories. One day, in a bookstore, I leafed through a book written by a psychic. She described how she would hold an object dear to the person who had come to her for a psychic reading. Then she closed her eyes and images drifted into her mind. Because she had been doing psychic readings for a long time, she knew how to interpret these images. For example, an engagement ring meant marriage in the future, or flags from various countries meant travel. The psychic's description of how the images came to her resonated with me. These images worked metaphorically, by connection, and through relationship.

One night in bed, with trepidation, I attempted to broach the subject with Max. I said, "I know this sounds crazy, but sometimes I think I can remember a time when you and I were married in a previous life."

Max misinterpreted my disclosure as an expression of my love for him. He patted my arm affectionately. "If I can have you for more than one lifetime, then I'm going to put in a request to have you in the next life too."

"Well, actually, I think maybe something happened between us in a past life that affects us in this one."

"Maybe I was Anthony and you were Cleopatra and we lived together in the ancient city of Atlantis." Max laughed as he kissed his finger and touched it to the tip of my nose. I dropped the subject.

Another time, I tried to open the conversation again. I asked Max what he thought about reincarnation. "Don't tell me you believe in that stuff," he scoffed.

If I pursued a discussion on this topic, I would clearly be perching precariously on the rim of credibility as far as Max was concerned. My Victorian memories were so important to me and yet I couldn't talk about them with him. I believed that I was remembering images and emotions from a former relationship between us that had a real and powerful impact on my present relationship with Max, yet his rigid dismissal of reincarnation or past-life memories prevented me from discussing any of it with him. Unable to talk with Max about this, how could I possibly work through it with him?

Subconsciously at first, but soon consciously, I began to squeeze Max out of my life. Sadly, he didn't notice the changes occurring in our relationship. When we made love, I fantasized exciting situations and imaginary partners in order to become aroused. I went far away in my mind while he touched me. Max never suspected; although I wished he would. I wanted him to notice something had changed. I wanted him to work with me to save our marriage.

My preoccupation with my own issues was interrupted abruptly when Papa had a heart attack. He suffered from angina and atrial fibrillation, for which he was on medication. I had not admitted to myself that my parents were aging, and that Papa's heart problems were bound to catch up with him as he got older. While Papa was in intensive care, his doctors, colleagues of Max's (with special instructions from Max to give Papa the finest medical attention), ran a series of tests and discovered he had diabetes. Papa returned home from the hospital weak and shaken. Mama put him on a restricted diet according to a plan drawn up by a nutritionist. He resigned from the board of directors at the temple and retired from the family business, although Uncle Izzie frequently called him to ask his opinion. He had always been so active and involved in the community that his sudden retirement depressed him. He didn't know what to do with himself. He was not the sort of person who could remain idle for long. His image of himself as hale and hearty had been blasted to bits.

I brought the boys to see him often because they cheered him more than anything else. Sarah had recently moved back to the East Coast from California and she took a week off work when Papa came home from the hospital to spend time with him. Rina and Arthur had gone to live in Africa for a year and I had an address for them but no phone number. I sent a telegram. If there was ever a time for Rina and Papa to call off the dogs and reconcile their differences, this was it, I thought. Sarah disagreed. She was of the opinion that communicating with Rina again might give Papa another heart attack. I wondered how a father and daughter could so completely cut each other out of their lives. I couldn't imagine keeping my sons apart from Papa.

The doctor said Papa could live for many more years on proper medication and by maintaining the recommended regimen of diet and exercise. But we could all see how dramatically he had changed after the heart attack. He seemed distracted and distanced. He sat still for long periods of time and we were not used to seeing him inactive.

The day before Joel's ninth birthday, Papa and Mama came over for lunch. We made party favors and decorations. Papa blew up two dozen colorful balloons and played with the balloons with the boys. They batted them in the air and tried to keep them all aloft at once, crashing into each other in their efforts. I played the balloon game with them. Papa seemed more like his old self. He played Parcheesi with Sam and Joel while Mama and I assembled party favor bags and made clever table decorations.

The next day, an hour before Joel's birthday party was to begin, Papa was reading the Sunday paper when he nodded off in his recliner. He had a second heart attack and died peacefully in his sleep. Sarah telephoned and told Max, who took me to our bedroom and broke the news to me as gently as possible. Looking back, I think I must have been irrational from the moment I found out. I decided I did not want to ruin Joel's birthday party, so I kept the news from the boys and orchestrated party games, cut cake, scooped ice cream, and tended to the needs of eight little boys for two hours. I came apart at the seams when the children began to leave and Joel wanted to give away the balloons. The balloons had Papa's breath inside them. I locked myself and the balloons in my bedroom. Max concluded the party, sent the guests home without balloons, and then explained to our boys that Grandpa had died. It was just as well that I had locked myself in the bedroom, because I was in no condition to cope with the wails of my children when they heard the news.

Alone in my bedroom, I unleashed my wrath in a diatribe against the doctors for not doing more, for not providing an effective medication, for not choosing to do bypass surgery, for not foreseeing the gravity of the situation and making a successful attempt to save Papa. I wanted to sue the hospital and Papa's cardiologist. I made up what I would say in court. I raged and fumed, alternately kicking the balloons violently and then drawing them to me and hugging them tenderly.

Max could not coax me to open the door. Joyce sent him away and then, speaking soothingly, as if convincing a psychotic to hand over a gun, Joyce gained admittance and sat with me as I talked through my anger and grief. Then, together, we stored the balloons safely at the back of my walk-in closet (out of sight). Joyce drove me to my parents' house.

During the funeral and the traditional Jewish week of mourning that followed, I leaned heavily on Max and he was completely there for me. I wandered in a fog of non-comprehension, unable to see or register the details that surrounded me. I held Papa's spirit near and feared that if I allowed myself to return to the routines of my everyday life, my father's presence would leave me completely. If not for Max's sensitive patience, I might have had a complete breakdown.

Rina did not come home from Africa. Even though I understood, rationally, that it was too far for her to come, too expensive, and that she would not have made it in time for the funeral (which was held within forty-eight hours of Papa's death in accordance with Jewish law); I was angry with her anyway for not being present for Mama and for me during that difficult time. I desperately wanted the family to be together; but we weren't, we hadn't been for a long time, and now we would never be together again.

In the weeks following Papa's passing, I spent hours walking around our neighborhood. I ran memories of Papa through my mind while I walked. I thought that if I could hold him in my memory accurately, then he wouldn't really be gone. Joyce cared for the boys while I was thus preoccupied. She helped them process their own loss and grief because I couldn't manage it. Max worried about all of us. Joyce told him to give it time. She seemed well-acquainted with the course of grief.

Finally, there came an evening when I sent Joyce out of the kitchen and cooked dinner myself. I prepared some of Papa's favorite foods. I set the fancy table in the dining room. Max, Joyce, the boys, and I ate there together. Sam and Joel regaled us with stories from their experiences at school. The dinner was a turning point for me. After that evening, I slowly began to recover. I agreed to take the seat on the board of directors at the temple that Papa had vacated. As I emerged from the fog of my own grief, I turned my attention to Mama, who had withdrawn into an alarming state of shock. Sarah moved in with Mama temporarily. Sarah and I grew closer through our efforts to help Mama make the adjustment to the loss of Papa as she reshaped her image of her own future. Papa's presence and his impact remained with us. Among other things, we saw his footprint daily in the actions and accomplishments of his grandsons.

After Papa's death, I made dramatic changes in my lifestyle. I quit taking the Pill and bought a diaphragm. I consulted with a nutritionist and adopted an entirely new approach to food. I insisted that the boys and

Max drink low-fat milk and I banned red meat from the kitchen. I read the labels on everything and rejected high-salt and high-fat items that I had bought regularly in the past. I pushed fruits and vegetables on the family with a vengeance. I joined a health club, where I worked out religiously three days a week. I lost weight, trimmed down, put on some muscle, and got in shape.

I don't think I would have completed law school after the loss of Papa if not for Max's meticulous care during those months when I was so fragile. But as I recovered from my loss, his coddling and fawning irritated me. As hard as Max worked at rebuilding the intimacy we had once shared, I worked at maintaining just the right level of distance to keep both my marriage and my privacy intact. I passed the Bar Exam on my first try. We officially became a two-career household when I landed a job with a small progressive law firm that, among other things, practiced immigration law.

From the outside, I suppose we looked like the perfect couple. The doctor and lawyer with our two beautiful, bright boys. We owned a lovely house maintained by our Haitian live-in.

We were pillars of the Jewish community. Many years later, when they were grown, Sam and Joel referred to the part of their childhood when I attended law school as The Ice Age. They could feel the coldness between their parents, even though Max was oblivious to it. They relied on Joyce's verve to warm them.

In the spring of my first year as a practicing lawyer, Max was invited to deliver a paper at an obstetrics conference in Chicago. He asked me to go with him, but I bowed out so he went alone. As soon as Max left, on a Sunday morning, I cleaned the house from top to bottom. Joyce and I even cleaned the back of the closets, the garage, and the laundry room. During the week that Max was gone, I made sure not to stay late at the office so that I could make it home in time to eat dinner with Joyce and the boys. Sam and Joel were in the midst of a Monopoly jag, so after dinner and homework, we sat down to an ongoing game that we had spread out on a card table in the living room. I put jazz on the stereo and traded in houses and hotels with my charming sons. Max usually called to say goodnight to the boys before they went to bed.

The night before Max returned, I reflected back over the week without him. I had been happier than I had felt in years. It was a different kind of happiness from the elation I had felt early in our marriage and it was not that sense of blessed happiness I had experienced when the boys were little. This was a more steady and comfortable happiness, a deep happiness that came from within and did not depend on anyone else. I didn't want Max to come back and shatter it. I missed having him there for the boys; but I liked having him at a distance.

I no longer wanted or needed a husband.

I can't remember asking for a divorce. We didn't file for divorce, in fact, until many years later, when Max wanted to remarry. He never understood what went wrong, although he finally recognized that it had gone wrong. Perhaps he wasn't as oblivious as I had thought all that time, perhaps he just didn't want to accept what was happening to us. For my part, I couldn't explain to him my perspective without discussing the relationship I had with him in a previous life as his abused Victorian wife. It was a key conversation that we would never have because he dismissed this very real part of my life as make-believe. And there was the heart of the whole disaster. If he had opened his scientific mind to the possibility of my visions and recollections, we might have had a chance at mending whatever had torn asunder in that former lifetime, and in the present one. Even if my Victorian memories were nothing more than a figment of my imagination, they were real to me, they were part of my framework of reality. And what we perceive is what is real to us. We create our own reality. Max could not erase my reality just by insisting that it did not or should not exist.

After Max moved out, I went through my clothing to cull out the old-style things, and I came across that teddy. I sat in a chair, closed my eyes, and threaded the silky undergarment through my fingers as I allowed the teddy to control my thoughts in the way that I had learned to extract meaningful images from objects. I saw myself in that same white-lace-curtained, dark-wood parlor that had so often appeared in my mind's eye. I sat at the card table, my corset too tight and my brain addled and dizzy. Victorian-Max glided up behind me and placed his hand on my shoulder, as if restraining me in that position and in that place. But, to his apparent astonishment, I rose and walked out of the room. I removed the corset, took the pins out of my hair, and changed into a pair of pants and a billowy blouse. Then I ran into a field of wildflowers and tall grasses where a breeze blew, a breeze of fresh, crisp air that smelled like line-dried sheets or the hair of a small child who has been playing outdoors. I was free.

I put the teddy in the giveaway clothing bag.

SHAYNA

For as long as I can remember, my greatest love has been the dance. My life would have been difficult had I not had talent. But I do. My body has ever been an instrument of the dance. I think of it as "the dance" as if it is my master, or perhaps my lover. From my first days studying ballet as a child, I worked hard to build the muscles necessary to allow me to serve the dance.

When I joined the National Ballet School, I knew I might have a future as a prima ballerina. But I did not allow myself to think about that. Instead, I focused on learning from my teachers and my peers, who were some of the finest dancers and choreographers living. I never expected to become famous. I expected nothing in particular. I simply wanted to dance. When I debuted in a principal role at the National, and made such a splash, I surprised myself more than I surprised the effusively flattering critics and the enthusiastic audiences.

My trademark as a ballerina became my ability to seemingly defy the laws of gravity. Images that audiences as well as photographers took away from my performances held me in mid-air, as if in flight. The newspapers nicknamed me "Oiseau," meaning bird. My mother speculated that the mad, terrible state of the world during my early years had left me with a subconscious desire to flee the planet and so I propelled myself airborne. She was wrong. I had no desire to flee and I did not recall my childhood as a dismal time in my life.

Once, a journalist asked me in an interview to share my first childhood memory. I told him, "My oldest memory is a birthday party held in my honor in Crevecoeur, where I was born and lived during the war. My Aunt Miriam, who the Nazis later murdered, decorated a pony cart with flowers. I remember the thrill of that pony cart. We sang and danced. I was given a bouquet of fragrant lavender and bright orange nasturtiums, a little wooden giraffe, and a dress with cherries printed on it that I wore constantly afterward." I thought this memory was an example of the delights of my childhood that I remembered. I did not dwell on the deprivations and horrors brought by the war. I have always had a positive attitude.

During my early years, I sensed the adults in Crevecoeur were filled with a pervasive sadness. I knew that someone had gone missing, that many people had gone missing; and that the adults in our village suffered for the loss. I believed these missing people lived beyond the fields and vineyards, like a rainbow standing in a meadow, appearing to be close enough to touch but unreachable. Despite the feelings of sadness and loss that surrounded me, I did not suffer for lack of wondrous things to brighten my childhood.

My playmate Isabel was raised with me as a sister, in the same house, and we danced, sang, told stories, and drew pictures together. We ran in the fields and orchards. We picked flowers and shouted at the neighbor's ducks. Isabel's presence anchors my recollection of the war years. We continue, even now, to help one another reconstruct our memories, comparing notes to distinguish between the real and the imagined.

When my father returned from the fight and my family moved to Paris after the war, we didn't have much money, but I never thought of myself as poor. Sometimes I wanted things I could not have. The thing I wanted most, however, was to dance, and this I had in abundance. I adored my adopted brothers from the moment they arrived. After living in a completely female household throughout the war, I had to adjust to living in a male-dominated household in Paris.

After I became a prima ballerina, journalists frequently referred to my "difficult childhood," meaning the conditions of the war, my father's imprisonment in Auschwitz, and the poverty of my family's early years in Paris. I do not remember anything difficult about my childhood. I had a wonderful childhood, embraced in the love of family and friends, which prompts me to ask: How does one define poverty?

Once I was accepted into the ballet program, my life revolved around the National. When I was fifteen, I met Vivian, my best friend. Viv grew up in Nice and had auditioned for the National every year for five years before she finally got in. Since I had been at the National for a few years by the time Viv arrived, I thought it my duty to explain to her what to expect and how things worked. We shared simple tastes, unlike many of the other, more pretentious girls, who often frustrated our teachers and choreographers with temperamental outbursts. Viv and I were not divas. We were workhorses. Even though we competed with each other for the best roles in the youth ensemble, our friendship never suffered and we supported and encouraged each other. We went everywhere together; to art shows, the theater, concerts, whatever we could get into free or on the cheap.

When Viv first arrived in Paris, she stayed with her cousin. Following a flurry of phone calls between my mother and Viv's concerned parents, she moved in with my family. My mother looked after Viv as if she was her own daughter. I remember her poking her head into our room to remind us not to stay up all night giggling when we had a strenuous day of dance ahead of us come morning.

The entourage of earnest and serious-minded young men from the Sorbonne, with their flat-footed attempts at flirtation, who continually followed my father around, offered us hours of entertainment. I was dedicated to my career and had no interest in a serious beau. Viv, who often said she was "just an old-fashioned girl," hoped to settle down with the right man eventually and raise a family, but certainly not before she had danced for a few good years. Her family plans exasperated me. "Why invest in this rigorous dance training if you plan to leave it in a few years to raise a family? That's a waste."

"How can it ever be a waste? I plan to enjoy every minute of it until I'm done. The lifespan of a prima ballerina is brief. I'll be finished by the time I'm twenty-five. Ballet is not my whole life. I have bigger dreams."

"Bigger? After you're too old for a principal role, then you can choreograph and perform in modern dance or jazz dance. It never stops. It just changes."

"I don't want to keep dancing forever. I want to have a normal life. Have children. I'm going to settle in a small town and open my own dance studio. Can you picture those sweet little girls in their tutus twirling around like sugar plum fairies?"

"Crashing into each other and falling over their own feet, you mean. No, I can't imagine throwing away so many years of training and hard work."

"Cheer up, Cherie, maybe I won't meet the right man for many years."

"Well you will not catch me raising a bunch of whining, snotty children."

"My children won't whine. They'll be adorable."

We graduated to the adult company together and made our debut in the same season. Viv's mother came from Nice to see her dance and she brought a garish bouquet of flowers to Viv in our dressing room afterward, where she cried like a histrionic soap opera star. We both sighed with relief when we put her on the train back to Nice. "I'm sorry Maman is so maudlin," Viv apologized to me and my mother as we departed from the train station. "She thrives on melodrama. Once you scratch the surface of all that fuss, you will find a remarkably sensible woman."

"Don't apologize for her," Maman instructed. "You've fulfilled her dreams for you and she has a right to express her happiness."

Viv and I had a glorious first season with the adult company. Isabel and Catherine came to Paris from Crevecouer on the train to see me dance. Everyone shared the excitement of my rave reviews and instant stardom. When Viv and I rented our own apartment in the Montmartre, we continued to go to my parents' house for Sunday dinner every week.

In the spring, a young scenic designer came to the National to design the sets for a new *Swan Lake*. Pierre emulated good health and had a fresh, wholesome face. He had cornflower blue eyes, straight sandy-brown hair, and graceful long fingers. Pierre was rather young to be designing for the National, but, at thirty, he seemed old to me and Viv when we met him at a cocktail party.

Viv and I stood off to the side, giggling and gossiping about the antics of the company members as we watched them become progressively more inebriated. Pierre approached and introduced himself to us and then we took it upon ourselves to brief him on the company dynamics and drama, regaling him with our tales about the people surrounding us at the party, as well as other characters at the National whom he had not yet encountered.

"We know these people much too well," I explained. "We're familiar with their foibles, failings, and peculiarities."

"And I suppose they are familiar with yours?" Pierre suggested.

Viv pushed her lip out with an air of superiority. "We don't have any failings and peculiarities."

"What do you have?" Pierre asked.

We replied in unison, "Passion for the dance."

Pierre asked us about ourselves, where we came from, why we had become dancers. As we talked, we drifted out into the garden, where we could smell the spring flowers and herbs beginning their summer's journey. We sat together on a low stone wall, Pierre in the middle, I on the left of him and Viv on the right.

"Tell us a joke," Viv demanded. "We want a good laugh, right Shayna?"

"Yes, we do," I confirmed.

Pierre rubbed his chin. "I can't remember any."

We studied him while he thought.

"I can't think of a joke with the pair of you staring at me like hungry tigers," he complained.

"Stop looking at him, Viv, you're making him nervous."

"Me?" Viv exclaimed in a mock huff. "Don't blame it on me."

"Oh, well, I remember a joke; here you go," Pierre said. Viv put her arm through his as we settled in to listen. "There was a man who had a girlfriend who was a social climber and she planned to have a fancy party. The day before her party, she asked him to bring her escargot to prepare for her guests. So off he went to the shop and bought a bucket of escargot. But when he came out of the shop he bumped into a beautiful woman who engaged him in conversation and, forgetting about the party, he went with her to a café and they spent the whole night…"

"This is a respectable joke, right?" I cautioned, with a twinkle in my eye.

"Of course," Pierre reassured me. "They spent the whole night talking."

"Now you've censored the joke," Viv complained.

I shushed her. "I want to hear how it ends."

Pierre continued. "The next day they went for a walk by the river. Suddenly, he realized that he had left his girlfriend high and dry without her escargot, and her party would be starting shortly. So he excused himself from the woman he had met and went to his girlfriend's apartment. When he reached the top of the stairs, he thought to himself that he had better come up with an explanation. So he threw the snails out of the bucket and onto the stairs before he knocked on the door. His girlfriend answered, dressed up for her party. She frowned at him in anger and demanded, 'What took you so long?' He then turned to the snails crawling on the stairs and said, 'C'mon, you guys, I said hurry up'."

We laughed and Pierre flushed with pleasure.

While Pierre remained in attendance at the National to work with the scenic shop as they built, painted, and mounted his sets, the three of us spent every evening together. At first we went out, but soon we simply stayed at our apartment, cooking together, playing cards, listening to music, and entertaining each other until we turned in for the night. Pierre often slept on the fold-out couch in the living room. Our friends at the National called us the "Three Musketeers."

Once *Swan Lake* opened, Pierre's business at the National was concluded. While he was still in town, he caught me alone and asked me to go to dinner with him.

"Just me? Viv's feelings will be hurt," I said, worriedly.

"The three of us have had some fun together and I expect we will have some more. But I'm asking you to go out to dinner with me; just the two of us. What do you think?" Pierre asked anxiously.

His proposal caused me to view him in a new light and he looked attractive in this new light. I accepted his dinner invitation.

When I broke the news to Viv, she was enthusiastic. "What a natural!" she exclaimed. "You two will be great together. You're already such good friends."

"We're just going to dinner," I reminded her.

"After dinner comes breakfast, then lunch, then dinner again. I can see the writing on the wall, Cherie."

Viv's prophecy rang true. In Pierre I found a companion who never resented sharing me with the dance. He had an artistic vocation of his own, so he understood mine. My parents approved of Pierre from the start. In addition to his talent and other positive attributes, he argued politics intelligently with my father, who took delight in bashing Pierre's more conservative views.

Soon after I met Pierre, I advanced rapidly in the adult troupe at the National. I stood out from my peers because I was willing to take risks physically and emotionally. Viv's fluid style was far more traditional than mine. She had immaculate technique and nearly hypnotized the audience. I, on the other hand, stunned the audience. I pushed my body to the edge of belief. I did not do well with ordinary. Ordinary bored me. I loved nothing better than a challenge. Pierre confided, "When I watch you on stage, you are a stranger, unfamiliar and surprising."

"When I'm on stage, I'm unfamiliar and surprising to myself. The dance creates what I become."

To celebrate our one-year anniversary, Pierre and I went to Italy for a week. We took the early-morning train from Paris. As the city dissolved into the countryside, I remembered the many hours of my childhood spent in the forests and meadows of Crevecoeur. We admired the splendid scenery as it flashed past the train windows; the fields of bright-yellow wild mustard flowers and the quaint cottages with storybook shutters and fairytale gardens. The scenery inspired Pierre. Just prior to our departure, he had been offered a job in London designing the sets for a production of Shakespeare's *As You Like It*. He took out his sketchpad as the train rushed through the pastoral landscape.

After we crossed the border into Italy, the motion of the train made me drowsy and I slept until we reached our destination. At the station, Pierre hailed a taxi to take us to our hotel. Just that fast we escaped to a place far away from everything familiar.

Pierre ordered beer and cold sandwiches from the room service menu and we ate in our spacious suite. We made love slowly in the fluffy hotel bed.

The next day I woke to clear sunlight cast on burnt-orange sunflowers in a powder-blue vase on the dresser. I stretched, catlike, in the comfy bed, feeling like royalty. When I opened the partially shuttered windows, I basked in the view of a lake nestled in the mountains. I adored the mystery of arriving in the dark and discovering in the morning that I was surrounded by beauty. The fresh air practically sizzled as it hit my lungs. I padded across the room and slipped back under the covers, where I cuddled into the warmth of Pierre's chest. We spoke softly in our eiderdown nest until Pierre grew restless and rose to shower, dress, and explore.

We were the last ones down for breakfast, so we had the small dining room to ourselves. We sat by the window and drank deep cups of strong Italian coffee. After breakfast, we went for a walk around the lake. Pierre discovered that he could rent a boat so he immediately bought a lime-green parasol for me, rented the boat, and rowed me around. "I have always wanted to row a woman with a parasol around in a boat," he confessed.

"You designed me into the scenery."

After we returned the boat, he shot pictures of me and my parasol dancing in the amber, late-afternoon light, weaving in and out of slender trees with white bark that made them look like chalk marks on the landscape. After a light supper, we strolled by the lakeshore. I paused to gaze up at the clear sky, sprinkled with stars. Pierre took me by the shoulders and turned me to him. I knew what was coming and I dreaded it.

"I want to marry you, Shayna."

"I know."

"There's more."

"I know there is."

"I want us to have a family together. Will you marry me?"

He knew I adamantly did not want children. He absolutely did. Perhaps he thought that he could change me. Perhaps he thought that a miracle would happen and I would have a new answer. But I had the same old answer. "I would marry you if you didn't mind not having children. But you do mind. You deserve children as much as I deserve to devote myself completely to the dance."

I sat on the low stone wall that ringed the lake and he sat next to me. We had reached this impasse before, but never so definitively.

"This decision will never change with me."

"What about adopting?"

"Dear, dear Pierre." I took his face in my hands that were so carefully trained to gracefulness. "I do not plan to live the kind of life that is good for raising children. I plan to travel, keep odd hours, have the freedom to run off on a whim. I will not stay with the National forever. I will perform and choreograph and follow the dance wherever it leads me. Children need to be put before everything else. I would never put a child before the dance."

"Then I will put our children before everything for both of us," Pierre pleaded.

"You know that children deserve better than that from a mother."

We gazed across the lake for a long time in silence. I curled into Pierre's familiar body, which smelled so fresh from the outdoors. He held me close. We savored the moment because we both knew that very soon I would release him to seek his heart's desire. I had found mine, and it did not reside with a man.

"There is something I always wanted to ask you," I said, breaking the silence. "Why did you choose me instead of Viv?"

"What do you mean?"

"Before, when the three of us were friends. There must have been a point at which you decided on one of us. Why me? Why not Viv?"

"Viv is comfortable. I could not become passionate about comfortable."

"You chose the wrong one. Comfortable makes a good wife. You know that if you keep seeing me, you will never get involved with someone else; someone who will give you those children and that house with the bicycles scattered on the front lawn."

Pierre took my hand in his. "I will always love you, my friend."

I shook his hand. "And I you. Friends, then."

We spent a bittersweet, peaceful week at the lake. It was our swansong. When we returned to Paris, we parted ways. Pierre went to

England to design his Shakespeare and then he went to America to design two shows in New York. Though neither Pierre nor I shed a tear over the split, Viv cried her eyes out. "You are so stubborn, Cherie," she complained. "You two were great together." Although I missed him, I sincerely hoped he would meet the right someone with maternal yearnings soon.

My parents were terribly disappointed that I split with Pierre; especially Maman, who wasted no time in chastising me for letting a catch like Pierre slip away. "Dance depends on the agility of the body," she lectured, "and that is a finite element. What will happen when you grow old and your body refuses to obey commands? I want you to be happy. I want you to find a husband who will travel through life with you."

"I hope to find a husband too. But he must be someone willing to take his place second in line to the dance. And I will never change my mind about children."

"The sort of warm, generous, and big-hearted man I would wish for you to marry will probably want children," she said, bemoaning my choice.

"There are many big-hearted men who can manage without children," I reassured her.

"When your youth fades, will you be satisfied choreographing and not performing?"

"Maman, you mustn't worry about me. Surely one day the aging joints of the Oiseau will drag her to earth. But I will never stop dancing. There's modern. There's jazz. I love to choreograph. Even when I stop performing, I will always dance. Dance is my life. Dance is my children."

"I want for you more than the adoration of fans. I want for you the circle of family."

"I'm truly touched by the sentiment. I'm not being facetious. But I have plenty of family already. There's you and Papa, Micah and Zac and their families, Isabel and her tribe in Crevecoeur. Lord knows she has enough children for us all. And my friends at the National, whom I have known since I was a child. There's Viv."

"I would like for you to have intimacy and the daily living with a husband."

"I would like that too, but not at the expense of what I hold most dear. I have known where my heart lies for as long as I can remember. The dance is the great point of light at the center of everything. I'm never as completely alive as I am when I am dancing. When I dance, I am pure spirit, burning brightly."

"Nothing else gives you that sense of burning brightly? Not family, not your participation in community, not making a contribution such as helping a child learn to read?"

"Aha! You see? Teaching is your vocation, not mine, and you're looking through the lens of your own perspective."

"Oh for goodness's sake!"

I wagged my finger at her. "Helping a child learn to read? The creative spirit, the spirit of the true artist, is not content with these pieces of everyday life, which are fodder for the art. Life serves art."

"I thought it was the other way around," Maman said, as she put her hand on her hip. "Most artists value their family and community above their art, and the art is work. Good, solid, rewarding work, but work nonetheless."

I jumped up and pounded the palm of my hand on the table. "I disagree. I'm fortunate in that I'm able to earn a living dancing, but few artists are able to do the same. Most artists must practice their art on the side, during their spare time. I feel sorry for those artists who must earn a living doing something else and are forced to find time here and there to do their creative work, which is their sustenance. And trust me when I say that they are driven to find that time because creating that art is imperative and inescapable. I believe art defines life."

"Art is a tool for change," Maman replied without hesitation.

"Spoken as a true political activist. But, really, don't you think it's more complicated than that? The art that endures is the art that contains the deeply human moment, that illustrates the universal condition of humanity, which has nothing to do with politics. It occurs in spite of politics. For instance, a poem written in Auschwitz is a message of universal human suffering that transcends the particular political situation."

"But what makes the poem poignant? What gives the poem power? Auschwitz, of course."

"What does it matter where the poem was written? If the poem cannot stand alone in its power, then it will not endure, no matter how poignant it may be in the moment. It must transcend the moment to endure."

"You could have been an attorney."

"I would never have been able to sit still long enough," I disagreed, with a laugh.

After my separation from Pierre, I went on a tour with the National. Meanwhile, Viv remained in Paris, and we kept up with each other by exchanging frequent postcards.

On that tour, I fell in love with Sweden and Sweden fell in love with me. In Amsterdam I worked with a dynamic, innovative choreographer, with whom I had a wild affair. I went out of my way to watch other dancers perform, particularly innovative modern dancers. While in Sweden, I saw Donya Feuer dance. I had been to see both Arlet Bon and Sara Pardo perform in Paris; and their brand of modern dance gave me exciting ideas for choreography. When my small window of opportunity as a prima ballerina closed, I would be prepared to transform myself and to branch out in new directions.

On my first night back in Paris from the tour, I dumped my suitcase in my apartment and ran out to meet Viv at a restaurant for dinner. As soon as we had ordered our meal, Viv said, "There's something I need to talk to you about."

"My goodness, Viv, you look so serious. Don't scare me. What is it? Tell me quickly."

"It's about Pierre."

"Is he alright?" I asked in alarm.

"Oh, yes, never better."

"Is he back in Paris?"

"Yes. Yes, he is."

"Did he get married or something?" I laughed.

"No, he's not married." Viv swallowed. "While you were away, Pierre and I went to a few shows and we had dinner together. Just like old times." It was at that point that I figured out what was going on. "You weren't here. I couldn't ask you how you might feel about it. I couldn't write it on a postcard. We've been seeing each other. Is that alright?"

"It's fine with me," I told her; and it really was. "I'm delighted. For both of you."

"You're my best friend." Viv reached across the table and took my hand. "I would never want a man to come between us."

"He won't," I promised. I could see the weight lift from Viv's shoulders.

"We have plans to go to Athens next week. He would like to see you before we go. I wanted to talk to you before he did."

"Let me get one thing straight, though," I said, in the most severe voice I could muster.

"What's that?" Viv asked anxiously.

"I want to be the maid of honor."

I did see Pierre before he took Viv to Greece; but it was hardly necessary for him to warn me that he planned to propose to Viv there. I knew him so well that I could figure out what the trip to Greece meant. Upon their return to Paris, Viv gave notice at the National without a backward glance. I did not understand how a gifted dancer could drop her career like that, but that was the difference between us, and that was why she was the right one to marry Pierre. They moved to suburban Bourg-la-Reine where Viv opened a ballet studio and taught little girls in pink hairbands how to point and turn. The following winter, Viv called to tell me that they were expecting a baby and they wanted me to be the godmother. I felt only the greatest delight and love for both of them as I moved on with my own life.

I have never regretted my decision not to have children. I had plenty of children in my life without having any of my own. I played the role of devoted auntie perfectly for Viv's children; as well as for Isabel's brood in Crevecoeur, Micah's two little girls, and Zac's rambunctious, athletic progeny.

My parents went to Zac's house for dinner every Sunday and I joined them as often as possible. They had wrested a comfortable life from the wreckage of the war. My father carved out a fine position for himself as a professor at the Sorbonne. He published a couple of books and he wrote a regular column in a widely circulated Socialist newspaper. Maman taught adult literacy classes at a community college. After I left home, she organized and participated in demonstrations, marches, rallies, and other political actions; advocating for the poor and the exiled and making a ruckus to promote social change. She was even arrested once for protesting the French involvement in Vietnam. I had to bail her out of prison.

My parents took it hard when the truth about the atrocities committed in the name of communism under Stalin came to light. The invasion of Hungary made Maman physically ill. (Zac's wife was Hungarian and she still had family there.) By the time the Berlin Wall went up and Solzhenitsyn's *A Day in the Life of Ivan Denisovich* appeared in French, my parents had left the Communist Party and reluctantly admitted that the practice of communism had irrevocably corrupted their original vision. My father joined the French Socialist Party. Maman had burned out on joining "isms" by that time and chose her causes and battles individually, until the Green Party emerged and she joined with a revitalized hope for the future. I had no interest in politics, which I'm sure annoyed my parents, but they didn't bother me about it.

I was delighted when my American cousin Rina visited Paris with her husband and daughter. After her visit to Paris, Rina struck up a correspondence with me, and whenever I went to New York to dance or choreograph, I stayed with her and her family.

One summer, I even suffered the heat of New York to collaborate on a project with Rina. I had an idea for a dance piece driven by a beat that had captured my imagination while watching dancers in the street. I didn't want to dance it, I wanted to choreograph it. I had seen Alvin Ailey's company perform and I had fallen in love with the look of his multicultural ensemble. I held auditions and assembled my own multicultural ensemble to perform my choreography. Rina designed the costumes and her husband brought in teenagers from Harlem to paint the backdrop. My young ensemble company embarrassed me with their worshipful excitement at the opportunity to work with me. We ran the show for ten weeks in a warehouse studio and earned excellent reviews. Working with Rina was the best part of the project. That dance piece broke a barrier for me professionally. I started studying jazz dance with a new dance coach when I returned to Paris.

A year and a half later, I returned to New York with more new ideas. Rina spent two months building masks to incorporate into my dances. I wore the masks, which had dynamic personalities, in front of mirrors as I choreographed moves that brought out the life in each mask. She and I devoured library picture books of African, Balinese, and Maori masks. I choreographed an evening of modern jazz entitled *Masquerade*. The dancers who had worked with me the year before returned to work with me again and I even performed in a couple of the pieces myself.

During my glorious, limited time as the Oiseau, I had traveled around the world performing. As I grew older, I continued to dance, but less and less in performance. I choreographed for the young talent coming up at the National. Age is not kind. I was often quoted in the media for saying "My true education in dance began when I left the stage."

One season, the National toured Israel, and I invited my mother to go along with me. We visited my grandfather where he lived on a kibbutz on the Sea of Galilee. The kibbutz was beautiful and the younger residents looked up to my grandfather, treating him with kindness and respect and taking care of him in his old age. He lived modestly. I flooded him with questions about my mother's childhood in Palestine and early years in Russia. I was grateful for that visit, since he passed away peacefully in his sleep the following year.

My grandfather's death reminded me that my parents were aging. I enjoyed watching my mother with Zac's children or Micah's girls as she sang them the same Russian songs, told them the same stories, and played with them the same quaint games that she had played with me and Isabel when we were young. I lived modestly and donated much of my money to charitable causes, including many arts organizations. I chose my friends for their candor, authenticity, creativity, and humor.

Over the years, I met, loved, and parted with a number of men. I lived with one of them for nearly four years. But I never experienced a sustained passion for any of them, and when they tired of my indifference they moved on. I preferred living alone. I had many friends, and more projects going at once than the New York Transit Authority. I adored traveling and collaborating with other choreographers, directors, and dancers.

I made a point of remaining in Paris, though, for the first Bastille Day celebration under the newly elected Socialist leader, Mitterrand. I would not for the world have missed my father's gleeful celebration party. My mother teased my father by referring to Mitterrand's ascension to office as "The Coronation." It might as well have been a coronation with that spectacular display Mitterrand staged on his first Bastille Day in office. My parents threw a Bastille Day party, for which my father festooned the house with red, white, and blue helium balloons. Party guests included their present and former students, their late-night-café friends, my mother's political activist comrades, and my father's colleagues from the Sorbonne. Of course, Zac and Micah and their families came. And I invited Viv and Pierre and the children. Party guests spilled out into the hot summer sun that baked the back yard.

I counted five languages spoken just within earshot as I perched on the windowsill and sipped ice water from a tall, green glass, which sweated and dripped onto the floor. My light cotton blouse clung to my skin. I noticed that my mother's mane of curly hair had gone almost entirely white and she squinted through amber, wire-rimmed glasses. My father's hair had turned baby-fine and silver. His eyes, though they still burned brightly, had faded in color. His shoulders stooped slightly. How much longer would I have them with me? Viv slid onto the windowsill next to me. "You look so serious, Cherie."

"I was remembering what my mother and father used to look like and realizing how much they've aged."

"I do that with the children. They grow so fast. I can't believe they're the same babies I nursed and tickled. The other day, I was upset because I couldn't remember the last time I changed a diaper on Stefan. I wish I had known it was the last time. One day I realized that the children had outgrown diapers and I hadn't used one in ages. I blinked and now I have a house full of teenagers. I wonder if I will know when I make love to Pierre for the last time."

"Don't get morbid," I warned. "How much have you had to drink?"

"Just a little champagne."

I took her glass away and set it on the table. "You know you can't hold your liquor and you get introspective when you drink. Enough."

As evening threaded the sky, my parents and most of the party-goers made a mass exodus via Metro to the light show and public celebration by the Eiffel Tower. Mitterrand produced an extravagant spectacle for his adoring followers. Slides were projected onto the buildings while music blared and hot-air balloons floated above the crowd. Once darkness fell, we were treated to a spectacular fireworks display. My father and his comrades danced and drank champagne with the crowd.

"He has waited a long time for such a day to arrive," Maman told me, with satisfaction.

"I hope Mitterrand lives up to his expectations."

"He won't. No leader ever does, and your father knows it. They all make mistakes. They all make compromises. They all answer to the money that put them in power. They are political creatures; corrupt to some degree or another. The simple fact of his election by the people is enough to sustain us for many years to come, no matter how Mitterrand performs."

Later that summer, Viv and Pierre took their three children on a family vacation to Crete. They returned home tanned, relaxed, and loaded with beautiful beach photos. The week after their return, Viv went in for a routine doctor's check-up and they found a lump in her breast. They scheduled her for a biopsy immediately, and swiftly diagnosed cancer. I had lived an orderly life until Viv's diagnosis. I had supreme control over my own fate, choosing each step in my illustrious career, choosing how I invested my energy. But this, what began to happen to my dear friends Viv and Pierre, and to their friends and their family; this I had no control over. I had forgotten the tenuous nature of happiness; that each of us lives always a hair's breadth away from losing what we hold most dear.

Viv underwent surgery and succumbed to chemotherapy; but the cancer spread to her lungs. I took a break from work to spend as much time as possible with Viv, Pierre, and their children. I camped out in the blue guest bedroom at Viv's and took on the role of live-in housekeeper. I soon discovered that Viv's youngest, Stefan, had a passion for cooking, and so we prepared gourmet dinners together for the family. It started out as an effort to entice Viv to eat, but soon evolved into a ritual that seemed to help Stefan, who was fifteen, deal with the pain of watching his mother die.

At the end, large-eyed and gasping for oxygen supplied by the tank next to her bed, Viv begged me to look after her family for her when she was gone. "Not so much the children," Viv instructed, "for they are resilient and stronger than they know. But Pierre. Promise me that you will look after Pierre, Cherie."

I promised.

When Viv finally slipped from her body, at home in her own bed, surrounded by her family and friends, Pierre said, "She has gone someplace where she can breathe."

I gently corrected, "She has gone someplace where she doesn't need to breathe."

Isabel came from Crevecoeur for Viv's funeral. She had known Viv only peripherally, but she came to support me through the ordeal.

"You know how we cheat death?" Isabel asked me, before answering the question herself without giving me time to reply. "We remember. The more we remember, the longer they live. The more memories of them we pass on to those who come after, the longer they live."

"Then Viv will live a long time," I responded.

True to my promise, I continued to spend time with Viv's family. Every Monday, which was dark night for the dance stages of Paris, I stayed in the little blue guest room at Bourg-la-Reine. I cooked something special for dinner with Stefan, who had decided to become a chef when he grew up. His older sisters, though busy with their own lives, made a point of eating at home on Monday nights so we could be together.

At first, Pierre could not find his way out of the maze of his grief. I would discover him sitting on the edge of his bed, stroking Viv's silky nightgown or standing in Viv's closet, breathing the scent of Viv's trademark jasmine perfume, which lingered there. He tried to give some of her clothes to me but I couldn't bear to take them. We had his daughters take what they wanted and then I cleared out Viv's clothing, jewelry, and other personal items. Pierre and I grieved together. Spending time with each other kept Viv close to us.

One moonless night, nearly two years after Viv's death, I went to Bourg-la-Reine to cook dinner with Stefan. When I arrived, Pierre explained that a friend of Stefan's had invited him to go to a concert and to spend the night in Paris. Stefan had expressed concern that he didn't want to disappoint me, but Pierre told him I wouldn't mind and sent him on his way. Stefan's absence left us alone for the night. We cooked a nice dinner together. We made chicken with a mushroom-and-cream sauce, asparagus with sesame oil dressing, and potatoes au gratin. We made fancy parfaits, with whipped cream and fresh raspberries, for dessert. We made an extra one for Stefan and left it in the refrigerator for him.

Pierre described the set design he was working on for a theater in Brussels. I had been invited to choreograph a jazz piece for the upcoming season at the National and I played a recording of some music I was considering. I wanted Pierre's opinion about it.

After dinner, we sipped chardonnay on the patio. Clouds sped across the sky and thunder rumbled in the distance. We stood side by side, elbows resting on the wooden railing, talking in hushed tones. I shivered.

"Cold?" Pierre asked.

"Just caught a chill for a moment."

Pierre put down his wine glass and wrapped his arm comfortably around my shoulders. He drew me into the circle of a warm embrace.

We stood like that for a few minutes, and then he kissed me, not innocently, as a friend, but on the mouth, with deeper intent. It seemed like an eternity had passed since we had last kissed in such a fashion, while at the same time it seemed that only a short time had passed since we had been lovers. The thunder sounded to me like laughter falling from the heavens.

I imagined Viv watching us and chuckling; whispering, "Of course. It makes perfect sense, Cherie." Given our history together, it did make perfect sense. We knew instinctively, as did Viv's children, that Viv would have approved. She would have wanted us to find happiness together, and to look after one another in her absence. And she would have thought it a good joke that in the end she saddled me with children, albeit grown-up ones.

The children insisted we get married, so we did. At our wedding, my mother put her arm around my waist and told Catherine, "You see how it is not over until it is over? If we live long enough, who knows what will happen?"

"That's the trick," Catherine replied. "To live long enough."

SARAH

I remember the day I met Ross in the parking lot at the zoo on the first of many joint family outings. We were four years old. The hot asphalt shimmered in the summer sun. Ross's baby sister sucked her fingers as she sat in her stroller and his mother offered oatmeal-raisin cookies to us from a turquoise tin. Later, Ross and I stood in front of the exotic bird aviary and watched the colorful creatures flit above while he licked a bright-green popsicle and I licked a bright-orange one. We touched popsicles and smiled conspiratorially, as if we had done something forbidden.

Ross and I started school in the same kindergarten. We sat next to each other at circle-time and sang "Itsy-Bitsy Spider," giggling as our fingers crept up our imaginary waterspouts. Throughout elementary school, Ross was my best friend.

One of Ross's family photo albums includes a picture of us "playing wedding." I am wrapped in a lace tablecloth and a chiffon scarf covers my hair while Ross is dressed in a white shirt with his clip-on bowtie askew beneath his chin. My hand is looped casually through the crook of Ross's arm and both of us wear serious expressions. Ross's mother won a photo contest advertised on the back of a cereal box with that picture. Her prize was a fancy new camera.

Ross had a talent for easing difficult situations with his sense of humor. After Grandpa died, the family gathered at Uncle Izzie's house each day to observe the weeklong formal period of mourning called *shiva*. When Ross's family paid their *shiva* call, Ross (who was twelve) regaled us with hilarious stories about Grandpa. He had that roomful of people who loved Grandpa dearly, and who would miss him terribly, laughing until it hurt. When the rabbi arrived to lead us in the recitation of the evening Mourner's Kaddish prayer, he found us holding our sides and gasping to catch our breath. The rabbi patted Ross on the shoulder and commented, "I see someone has already consoled the mourners, without the need for my ministrations."

When we turned fourteen, Ross and I officially started going steady. In some ways we were an odd pair since I needed a lot of private, contemplative time alone, while Ross thrived in social situations. During our high-school years, we had a tight circle of friends with whom we went to the movies and the pizza parlor, rode bikes, went swimming or skating in season, listened to music, and played board games. Ross and I frequently took the train into Manhattan, both with or without our friends, to enjoy city activities such as cultural events.

The issue of sex bubbled to the surface along with our hormones and we dipped our hands in the honeypot together. I took care of the birth control. Our clandestine encounters left me feeling smug, as if I had a delicious secret. Ross was worried that people would find out and our reputations would be sullied.

"How will they find out?" I asked him. "Who will tell?"

One night, during the summer before we left for college, we parked Ross's father's car at the municipal park and made love in the back seat until a flashlight cast its beam in the window. A policeman, who was the father of a friend of ours, escorted each of us home. Ross was mortified. I was furious because I had cherished the secrecy of our encounters. Papa was out at one of his meetings that night. Mama was surprisingly amused. The impropriety of the situation irritated her; but the manner in which we had been caught apparently provided her with something to laugh about. "I certainly hope you're using birth control," she said, in as stern a voice as she could muster, and clearly expecting a reply.

"Of course, Mama. I'm not foolish. I'm going to college before I get married and have children."

"When do you intend to tell your father what's going on?"

"Do I have to tell him?"

"Do you expect me to keep quiet? You must realize that your father's buddies at the police department will inform him in no time and I think he would prefer to hear his own business at home first."

"I don't know what to say to him," I mumbled, staring at my sandals.

"You should have thought of that beforehand," Mama pointed out, before relenting. "Alright, I'll tell him. But don't go parking out there again." She waved her hand in a gesture encompassing the wide and dangerous world beyond her four walls. "As long as you're using birth control then you and Ross might as well sleep together in the house. I'd rather have you safe at home."

The following evening, I was drawing a still-life of Mama's red summer roses, which I had arranged in a fluted crystal vase, when Papa knocked gently on my partially open door and entered.

"May I sit down?" he asked. Oh no, here it comes, I thought.

He sat on the edge of my bed, folded his large hands in his lap, and examined his feet until the silence became uncomfortable. He looked at the flower arrangement on my desk. "Your mother just asked me if I had seen that vase."

"I should have told her I was borrowing it."

"Very nice arrangement. You have your mother's touch." He paused. "Your mother tells me you're not a virgin."

This was an absurd conversation and I wished I could escape it, but it lurched forward flat-footedly with a life of its own. "She's right."

"I had hoped you and Ross would wait until you got married."

"I guess we didn't."

"I guess not. Things were different when I was a young man." I wondered if he ever wished he had sons rather than daughters.

"I'll tell your mother that you're drawing her vase," Papa said, as he stood abruptly and fled the room. He never mentioned my sex life again, even though Ross frequently spent the night at our house after that.

Ross subscribed more to Papa's way of thinking than Papa would ever know. He tried to talk me into marrying him throughout our senior year in high school, but I wasn't ready to get married. He assumed that we would go to the same college together, and when I didn't cooperate with his plans, he realized that he shouldn't assume anything about me, even though he knew me well. I emphatically did not want to get married right out of high school, and I did not want to go to the same college as Ross. I wanted to spend some time on my own, independent of my parents and independent of Ross; and I figured that my college years would be my only opportunity to do so. My parents agreed to pay extra for me to have a private dorm room so Ross and I would have some privacy when he came to visit me.

I never admitted to Ross that I regretted falling in love when I was so young. I wondered what it felt like to step out into a world of infinite possibility and while I loved Ross, I longed for a taste of that possibility.

On a crisp, scarlet-and-gold October day in the heart of apple-picking season, I sat on the front steps of my dormitory at Vassar and waited for Ross, who had taken the bus to come see me. A psychology textbook lay open in my lap, but I couldn't concentrate. The dorm faced a quadrangle carpeted by a lawn and bordered by well-tended flowerbeds, virtually empty and shut down for the winter. Along one edge of the lawn, flashy maples displayed their fall colors. I had seen the gardener planting bulbs earlier that week and had stopped to chat with him. I looked forward to the display his bulbs would provide in April.

Ross rounded the corner of one of the buildings, a small rucksack on his back and a slip of paper in his hand. He examined the paper and looked up, squinting into the late-afternoon sun as he ran one hand through his sandy hair. I stood and waved. Ross caught sight of me. Like a curtain brushing aside to reveal a breathtaking view, Ross's face opened into a delighted smile. We had never been apart as long as this before. He caught me in a playful hug and kissed me. I didn't know anyone in the world as well as I knew Ross, not even my own self. We stashed Ross's rucksack in my room and I took him to an Indian restaurant I had recently discovered. Over dinner, Ross made me laugh with his comic descriptions of his professors and classmates.

"I'm glad you're enjoying Princeton."

"If only you were there, it would be perfect." I had been accepted at Princeton, but I didn't go mainly because that was where Ross was going. "I miss you," he said mournfully.

"Absence makes the heart grow fonder."

Honestly, I hadn't missed him that much, but there was no reason to hurt his feelings by telling him this. I was enjoying having more time to myself; time not filled up with activities and conversation, time to sit alone in my room and read, draw, and meditate.

Back at the dorm, we spent a quiet evening talking, playing cards, and making love. Ross held me while we slept in my narrow bed. I snuggled into his arms. I did miss sleeping with him.

By Sunday, when Ross prepared to leave, I wondered if maybe I had made the wrong decision after all when I went to school so far away from him. "I don't want you to go," I told him, and I meant it.

"You can transfer after freshman year," Ross suggested hopefully. "You were accepted to Princeton once before."

"I'll take it under advisement." Maybe I would do it.

I walked him to the bus stop, where he would catch a local bus to the Greyhound terminal. We sat on a bench together and giggled, like a pair of mice in a hole, oblivious to the outside world. When the bus arrived, Ross bent me backward and kissed me like a soldier going off to war. Once he was gone, I walked back to my room, eager to return to my solitude. I couldn't reconcile my love of spending time with Ross with my craving for time alone.

During my freshman year, I walked around the campus by myself a lot, enjoying my anonymity. I went on a jag of reading about Buddhism. I visited Ross at Princeton a couple of times, but usually he came to see me at Vassar. When school finished in the spring, I moved back home, where I noticed a subtle change in my parents. They were noticeably more intimate with one another and they seemed to have slowed down.

Mama had converted Rina's bedroom into a sewing room. She had the room re-papered so that bright-yellow sunflowers and tiny blue forget-me-nots twinkled out of a creamy off-white background on the upper half of the walls and a blue wooden chair rail ran around the middle of the walls. Below the chair rail was blonde wood paneling. With windows facing south, the room was flooded with sunlight. Mama had placed her sewing machine in a spot that afforded her a view of the back yard; and a large, raised work table stood in the center of the room. She stored the materials for her many projects in plastic boxes lined up in neat rows on shelving that Papa had built into the wall for her.

Her projects had recently become a lucrative business. Mama designed and made hats and dresses, which she sold on commission out of a local dress shop. Because of her growing reputation, women approached her to design custom clothing for them. She had constructed gowns, cocktail dresses, and two rather elaborate wedding ensembles. An all-girl rock band out of New York had discovered her and she made all their show costumes. I thought that was pretty funny. It surprised me to realize that Mama had deferred this prolific creativity in order to raise us girls.

I spent that summer working in Aunt Malka's deli and saw Ross every day. He had a summer job near home too. We rode bikes, swam, read books aloud to each other, and made love through the hot summer nights in my little-girl bedroom with the dusty-rose tulip stencils on the walls. I drew flowers, took a yoga class, and played board games with Ross and my high school friends.

In the fall, when I returned to Vassar, I took a course in childhood development that required me to work two afternoons each week in the toddler room at the campus Early Childhood Development Lab. I adored those little faces that provided a window into those inquisitive toddler minds as they made sense of the world.

I discovered a Zen center and began attending an evening class there. My daily meditation kept me centered.

Meanwhile, Ross declared his major in physics and his courses were challenging. He did not visit me at Vassar as often as he had the previous year, although he called frequently. I looked forward to his calls and missed seeing him. I applied to Princeton as a transfer student, but I didn't tell anyone. I imagined how pleased and surprised Ross would be if my transfer worked out.

I envied Ross his friends at Princeton, because I had not made any real friends at Vassar. I had acquaintances, but no one I thought of as a friend in the same way that I thought of my high school friends. I decided in my sophomore year that my loner lifestyle was unhealthy, so I made an effort to cultivate friendships with a few of my acquaintances. There was a woman in my childhood development class named Peggy, who always seemed to be the life of the party. I figured that if I befriended her then she would connect me to a lot of other people. For instance, if a group of students from our childhood development class was at the library studying, Peggy might drift through, whispering in everyone's ear, "Let's go out for a root beer float, we deserve it." She had a way of getting something started.

Peggy, who planned to become a kindergarten teacher, worked with me at the Child Development Lab. Her contagious upbeat energy transformed even the most subdued children into gleeful playmates. She seemed to have piles of friends already, but she generously managed to fit me into her busy schedule. We went to the IHOP together once or twice a week and we ordered stacks of golden pancakes with whipped butter and maple syrup. Getting to know Peggy was a new friendship experience for me because my other friends had known me for my whole life. When I told her about my family, I found myself thinking about my family in new ways. Peggy and her eight siblings grew up all over the world, since her father served in the air force. She told the most entertaining stories about her childhood. I wanted to meet her mom so I could see for myself what kind of woman could survive the antics of that exuberant brood of children.

Ross and Peggy took to each other from the moment they met. In fact, when the three of us got together, I could barely squeak a word in edgewise. One weekend in February, Ross brought his softball and mitts with him when he came to visit from Princeton because there was an unusual mid-winter thaw. He, Peggy, and I headed to the park. When a gaggle of children turned up, I swiftly found myself up to my eyeballs in a lively softball game. Afterward, Peggy transformed herself into a growling beast and chased a herd of delighted youngsters around the playground while Ross and I sat on a bench and watched.

"She's really something else," Ross commented.

As darkness fell, we went back to my dorm room and made blueberry Pop-Tarts in my toaster. Peggy entertained Ross with stories about the children at the Child Development Lab. She told him about the boy who said he wanted to be a dinosaur when he grew up and the girl who had three goldfish, all named Mathew.

"You need some children of your own," I told Peggy jokingly.

"There will be plenty of time for that after I finish school," she replied.

"You need a husband first," Ross pointed out, as he grinned that lopsided grin of his that I loved.

Peggy stared in awkward silence at her Pop-Tart.

Ross looked at me over Peggy's lowered head and shrugged questioningly, as if to ask "What'd I do?" I quietly put my finger to my lips to prevent Ross from speaking.

When Peggy looked up, she studied us thoughtfully. "There's something about me I think you should know." A note of fear edged her voice. "I'm a lesbian."

"Is that all?" Ross blurted. "I thought you had a contagious disease or something."

"It's not contagious," Peggy responded with a dim smile.

"So I guess you need a girlfriend, not a boyfriend," Ross proposed, a little too gallantly. I knew he was not as comfortable with this revelation as he pretended to be.

"I want to be a teacher and I don't want anything to get in the way of that. Many people assume that if you're homosexual then you're a perverted child molester so I don't share that fact about myself much."

Ross nodded and closed his fist over his heart. "Your secret is safe."

Later, in bed, Ross said, "It's not that I'm judging her. It's just that I don't get it. I can't imagine how a woman could feel satisfied having sex with another woman."

"You don't like the idea of women satisfying each other sexually without you guys. It leaves you out of the loop."

"Not true," Ross protested. "I just can't imagine it."

"It's not so hard to imagine."

After Peggy's disclosure, my relationship with her changed. I had never known a lesbian before. She had piqued my curiosity. I wondered how she went about meeting other lesbians and how she went about going on a date. How did she separate feelings for her women friends from feelings for women she might be interested in romantically? The few times that I plucked up the courage to ask Peggy a question about her sexuality, she answered curtly and with obvious reluctance.

One Saturday evening we went to a concert together and, as we slowly worked our way across the crowded lobby toward the double doors of the auditorium, Peggy placed her hand in the small of my back to keep us from being separated in the crush of people. I was careful not to give any message with my body, but because I knew about Peggy, her hand burned electric through my clothes. I thought about that touch a lot afterward and from then on I was awkward around Peggy. I feared I might say something stupid so I tried not to say much at all. I avoided her, while thinking about her constantly.

My acceptance to Princeton arrived in the spring. They offered me a tuition scholarship only. At Vassar I had a full scholarship, which included my room and board, but I knew that my parents would support a transfer if I chose to do it and that they would pick up the additional cost. I still hadn't mentioned to them or to Ross that I had even applied and I held off on telling them that I had been accepted. I couldn't decide if I actually wanted to transfer to Princeton and I felt confused about why I couldn't decide. I sent in the deposit as if I was going, but I didn't burn my bridges at Vassar.

There was a philosophy course I wanted to take during the summer term, so I decided to stay at Vassar to do that. Peggy planned to stay on campus during the summer to do an intensive Spanish language program, and although I told myself that Peggy's plans had nothing to do with mine, I couldn't quite convince myself that was true, even though I hardly saw her anymore.

I went home for a couple of weeks between the spring and summer semesters. Ross and I rode our bikes together and went into the city to visit art museums. I felt distanced from my life and guilty for keeping the news about Princeton to myself. I could see that my reticence worried Ross, but typical of our relationship, he left me alone until I was ready to share whatever I had on my mind. I never did. The night before I left to spend the summer at Vassar, we made love especially slowly, gently, carefully; and I cried afterward.

"What is it?" Ross asked.

"It's nothing," I reassured him.

"I wish you would talk to me."

"I'm just feeling sentimental."

As soon as I returned to Vassar, a heat wave grabbed the region by the scruff of the neck. The thick, moisture-laden air had a character all its own. Walking felt like cutting through damp towels. I had to buy myself a fan because my room had no air-conditioning. At night I lay naked on top of my sheet and put a cool washcloth on my forehead. The dense air didn't move. During the day I did as little as possible. I couldn't eat, and instead drank a lot of water and juice. After three days of unbearable humidity, the sky filled with heavy dark clouds puffed to capacity with moisture. I watched from my window, anticipating the rain that would sweep through at any moment. Thunder boomed like a boastful lion. Lightening flashed.

There was a knock at the door and I answered to find Peggy holding a string bag full of purple grapes. Peggy's straight, thin bangs stuck damply to her forehead even though the rain had not yet begun. Her flame-red hair practically sparked with electricity and her deep-green eyes penetrated my reserve.

"Can you believe this weather?" Peggy asked. "Not even a breeze at night. I don't know about you, but I've lost my ability for logical thought. I hope this storm is the end of it."

I stood dumbstruck in the doorway.

"May I come in?" Peggy prompted me.

"Of course." I stepped aside to allow Peggy access.

"I just bought these; they're cold and seedless," Peggy said, referring to the grapes. I nodded, wishing I could stop feeling so self-conscious.

Peggy sat on the edge of my bed. "What's wrong?" she asked.

"The heat," I said, trailing off as I waved my hand.

Peggy studied me for a long moment. "You've been avoiding me."

I blushed with confusion.

A gradual smile slowly spread across Peggy's face. "You have a crush on me, don't you?"

I bit back tears and said nothing.

Peggy put the grapes down carefully on the night stand. She walked over and stood in front of me, like a giant question mark in the middle of my room. I took a deep breath and placed my trembling hands on either side of Peggy's neck and then I kissed her. Peggy kissed me back in a way that I had always wanted to be kissed but hadn't realized I wanted until it happened. I had imagined kissing Peggy, but never thought it would actually happen. She took me one step further, and then another, giving me time to adjust until, as if caught in a strong undertow, I lost my footing and was swept out to sea. Then I took the lead in our lovemaking with greedy desire.

We made love through the violet evening as the storm energetically unfolded outside with force and clatter, drenching the landscape with wave upon wave. As night fell, the rain withdrew and the air cleared, becoming crisp, fresh, and light after dropping its load of moisture.

The depth of passion that I experienced making love to Peggy surpassed anything I had ever felt when making love to Ross, much as I loved him. Ross had definitely given me pleasure. Our lovemaking had been an extension of our abiding friendship. But with Peggy, I was transported, re-made, and shaken brilliantly awake. I lost control and wandered in a mysterious labyrinth, which I neither could nor cared to escape.

The cool grapes Peggy brought were warm by the time we ate them as we faced each other on the narrow bed, our legs entwined, our breasts touching, wrapped in a golden after-glow.

My peaceful, orderly life exploded into a million tiny pieces that floated down around me like snow, even though I had never felt more alive or happier. How could I begin to explain this to Ross? I couldn't hurt him like that. I just couldn't. And in an agonizing flash I wondered, what about my parents?

The complexity of the situation paralyzed me and I did nothing. Meanwhile, I couldn't get enough of Peggy, who seemed both amused and aroused by my confusion. She gave me the space I needed to sort out my thoughts and feelings.

I officially turned down the scholarship to Princeton, finally confessing to myself that I had dragged my feet about it because of Peggy. I avoided going home to visit all summer, thinking up one excuse after another. Papa called several times to ask why he hadn't seen his "special girl." I felt guilty and missed seeing him and Mama, but I didn't think I could hide the fact that something miraculous had happened, something I couldn't share with them. I wasn't sure how Mama would react, but I felt sure from what had happened with Rina that Papa would refuse to tolerate what he would view as deviant behavior, even though I was his beloved baby daughter. I loved him too much to risk losing him. Would I have to spend the rest of my life concealing my truest self from my parents? I didn't think I could bear that, or successfully pull it off.

Ross called frequently, eager to visit me, and I cooked up creative and convincing excuses for him not to come. He could not be dissuaded indefinitely, however, and eventually he called to say he was on his way.

I panicked.

"What am I going to tell him? I'm ruining his life," I told Peggy.

"He'll bounce back," she replied, attempting to reassure me.

"He's going to want to sleep with me and I'm not into boys anymore."

"Are you sure about that? This is pretty new to you. Maybe you're interested in both of us."

"I don't think so," I answered woefully.

"Well, consider this an opportunity for you to find out for sure," Peggy told me, with a Buddha-like smile.

"You don't mind?"

"If you sleep with him? No. I don't own you. I'll make myself scarce for the weekend. It would not be good for the three of us to get together."

I was grateful for Peggy's attitude and wondered if I would be as magnanimous if Peggy wanted to have an affair with a man. But of course Ross was not an affair. He was a longstanding relationship going back as far as I could remember. There would be his anger to contend with and that scared me.

The day before Ross's visit, I was so anxious I couldn't eat. I wondered if I should tell him as soon as he arrived and get it over with. I imagined giving him a hug and saying, "Thanks for coming. It's great to see you. I'm a lesbian now."

When Ross finally did arrive, he gave me a hug and a kiss as usual, and proceeded to regale me with his humorous stories. I wished he was simply my best friend and had never been my lover. In a different reality, I would have turned to him for help figuring out how to deal with my present situation. I had no one to talk to about my relationship with Peggy.

We went to a pizza place for dinner. I forced myself to savor what would perhaps be my last evening with my dearest childhood buddy. I would break his heart later. We walked back to the dorm through the fragrant summer evening. He took my hand.

Back at the dorm room, Ross attempted to kiss me, but I was wooden.

He sat in my desk chair. "OK, Sarah, what's going on? Talk to me."

Sitting on the edge of my bed and wringing my hands with anxiety, I told him I had changed. I had learned something new about myself. "I've discovered that I like women. I mean, I'm a lesbian," I confessed barely audibly.

"Are you sleeping with someone?"

"Does that matter?"

"You are, aren't you? Do I know her? Of course I know her. It's Peggy, isn't it?"

I stared at the floor.

"She seduced you, didn't she?" He interrogated me with fury.

"I fell in love with her. It was mutual."

"And you suddenly don't want to sleep with me anymore? Because I'm a guy? Are you crazy or what?"

"I don't think that I ever wanted to sleep with a guy." No sooner had I said the words than I wished I could take them back. My thoughts were coming out all wrong.

"So you never wanted to sleep with me? I had the impression you enjoyed having sex with me."

"I did. Please don't be angry. I didn't do this on purpose. It just happened. You're my best friend in the whole world and the last person I would ever want to hurt. I can't help what happened. I've discovered that I'm not who I thought I was. I need my best friend as much as ever."

"So I've been downgraded to your best friend?"

"This is so hard to explain. But I'll try. With you, I feel like a forever friend, like you're my brother or something. Like we grew up together. You know me better than anyone does. When we make love it's, well, comfortable. Familiar. It feels good. But when I make love to a woman..."

"To Peggy, you mean," Ross interrupted. "This is not abstract, Sarah. She's a particular person."

"OK, to Peggy. When I make love to Peggy, it's both a sensual experience and a spiritual experience. I'm transported out of my ordinary self. My ordinary self dies and comes back different. Each time, it comes back different. It's like she's not a particular person when we make love; she's all women and I'm all women, and our passion is more than just the two of us." My description felt so lame. I doubted I could ever describe in words how I felt about Peggy and the ways in which my relationship with her was more powerful for me than my relationship with Ross.

"And you never experienced that with me?"

I knelt at Ross's feet and took his hands in mine. "I have loved you. I still do. I have enjoyed having sex with you. I probably still would. My spirit is touched by our friendship. But my spirit is not touched by our lovemaking. My spirit is touched, no, my spirit is moved, deeply moved in a powerful way I can't describe, when I make love to Peggy."

"So you and I are? What are we? Over?!" Ross asked incredulously.

"I don't know what we are," I answered miserably. "But we're not lovers." There, I had said it.

"I suppose this means I'm sleeping on the floor," Ross responded, with his characteristic humor.

"No. No. I'll sleep on the floor." The guilt I felt was unbearable.

"That was supposed to be a joke."

"Are you OK?" I asked, which was such a stupid question, but I couldn't think of anything else to say.

"No, I'm not OK. Everything is not OK. But frankly, my opinion is that you're going through a phase and I'll just have to deal with it." I hated his patronizing tone, but I decided to keep my thoughts to myself. I didn't want to make matters any worse. I would take anything he dished out that could help me get through the weekend with him.

Ross slept in his clothes on top of the blankets next to me. We didn't actually get much sleep. How could we? We talked, as Ross tried to process the change in our relationship. I didn't want to lose Ross as my friend and would have done anything to prevent that.

When he left the next day, we had not discussed how to present the situation to our families; although I had been clear about the fact that I didn't want my parents to know about Peggy. I would later discover that while I thought I had split up with Ross, he didn't perceive it that way. He believed that when I "got over this lesbian thing" (as he thought of it), he would pick me up and put the pieces back together. He knew Peggy well enough to have a sense about her child-like nature and he thought she would never make a commitment to a relationship with me. He believed that I would want a commitment. But it was the old Sarah who valued the comfort of commitment and I was the new Sarah, the one he didn't recognize. Commitment had dropped to the bottom of my priority list, at least for the time-being.

Ross called me upon his return home to inform me that he had told his parents and mine that I had asked him for a trial separation. I waited for Ross to go back to Princeton before visiting my parents at the end of the summer. According to Papa, Ross said that I "needed some space." The paternalistic buddy-buddy attitude of Papa and Ross irritated me, but Ross's version of what had happened made the situation easier for me to handle with my parents so I chose not to refute it.

By autumn, Peggy and I wanted to move in together, but we had to figure out how to arrange this discreetly because I was determined to hide our relationship from my parents. Just before Thanksgiving, Peggy found the perfect living situation. She answered an ad in the newspaper for house parents at the Mother Goose Children's Home. The ad said "couple preferred, singles OK." The director of Mother Goose needed to hire staff to cover certain night and evening shifts during the week and some weekends. It was a live-in situation. Peggy and I, both majoring in elementary education, presented an excellent interview.

While I was home for Thanksgiving, I had to listen to Sophie and Mama complain at length about Rina spending Thanksgiving with her friends instead of our family. I found myself defending Rina and secretly wondering if I would be so welcome in coming years if my secret was discovered. I couldn't imagine being left out of family celebrations.

On the day before Thanksgiving, I played a wild game of Clue with Papa, Sophie, and Max. Sophie was pregnant, and she and Mama talked endlessly about babies. I felt guilty for being so preoccupied with my own life and not communicating more with my sister during her pregnancy, so I was pleased to have the opportunity to feel her belly and share in her excitement. Papa was adorable in his delight at the prospect of becoming a grandpa. Sophie and I helped Mama with her holiday baking. Aunt Ida, Uncle Izzie, and my cousins joined us for Thanksgiving dinner. It was a relief to participate in all these ordinary activities with my family, far from the frightening complexity of romantic entanglements.

I carefully avoided speaking about Ross while I was at home. After the holiday, I returned to Vassar and moved into a large attic room at Mother Goose with Peggy. If someone had told me a year before that I, who cherished my privacy, peace, and quiet, would move into a Children's Home for a live-in, part-time job, I never would have believed them. Mama and Papa were baffled. I was deliriously happy.

I went to class during the day and in the evening I helped youngsters do their homework, then played card games, board games, and Ping-Pong with them. After the children went to bed, I studied for my classes in our attic hide-away. Peggy socialized much more than I did. It was a wonder she ever finished her school work. In fact, Peggy was a wonder to me in every way. Sometimes, Peggy and I pretended that the whole children's home belonged to us alone.

I learned so much more at Mother Goose than I would have learned from simply reading child development textbooks. I applied my school learning to my work at Mother Goose, and I learned from watching Peggy in action. Her humor, and her innate ability to help children work through their anger or defiance, defused many a sticky situation. I discovered my own strengths and weaknesses when it came to working with children. I could often intuitively read children's moods and feelings, and this sixth sense helped me to say or do just the right thing to help children survive their messiest emotions gracefully. Sometimes the right thing was Peggy's silliness. We made a good team.

In February I went home for a long weekend to see my new nephew. I felt a pang of envy for my sister's "normal" lifestyle, with her successful doctor husband who supported her and her baby boy. I wondered if I would ever secure a version of that comfortable, happy family life for myself. I wanted it with all my heart, but was not sure it was possible for someone like me.

Over spring break, Peggy decided that the recreation room needed repainting and that this fact afforded an opportunity to give the children an art lesson. Peggy talked a local paint store into donating the paint and a local hardware store into donating the brushes, drop cloths, and other materials. Peggy and I cleared the furniture out and primed the room white. Then Peggy brought the children in, one age-group at a time, and assigned them each a different wall, where they painted murals. I spent my break spotting the youngest children on ladders while they painted exotic birds into the tops of jungle trees and looking through picture books of coral reefs and ocean creatures with teenagers. The north wall dissolved into an alien planet designed by the seven-to-ten-year-olds. The end result was spectacular. Peggy had blue paint in her hair for nearly a week afterward. She wore it like a badge of honor.

The night before we returned to school to finish the spring term, Peggy and I sat alone in the revitalized recreation room and admired the children's work. I pointed out that we could actually read the developmental stages of the children in a million ways on the walls. Together we identified different aspects of children's growth as depicted in the murals. The following year, I would use photographs of the murals as the basis for my honors thesis.

I learned how to make fudge in large quantities. I learned how to make play dough from flour, water, and salt. I saw every imaginable mess that children could make with their food at the dinner table, particularly vegetables. I made buckets of applesauce with the help of many little hands. I made three different kinds of jam and ten kinds of soup. I became addicted to Saturday morning cartoons, evening sing-a-longs around the piano, and, heaven help me, chocolate-chip cookies made with M&Ms.

I saw what happens to children who have been neglected, abused, or unloved. I learned how to restrain children who were in danger of injuring themselves while having a tantrum. I witnessed how the legal system does and does not provide for the best interests of children from messed up families. I talked a fifteen-year-old girl into surrendering a knife without stabbing anyone. I helped a ten-year-old boy conceal the fact that he still wet the bed in fear the night before his court-mandated visit with his father. I prevented a child who had been raped from molesting another child. I made up my mind at Mother Goose that I would dedicate my life to making a difference in the lives of children. Teaching became more than a profession for me, it became a vocation.

I lived at Mother Goose for half of my junior year and all of my senior year of college and it was one of the happiest times of my life. Peggy and I both planned to stay in school for a fifth year to obtain our teaching credentials and I assumed we would continue to live at Mother Goose together. Then, three weeks after graduation, my world imploded.

Peggy announced she had met another woman and she packed up her things and moved out. Just like that. No discussion. I felt stupid, betrayed, hurt, humiliated, furious, blindsided. Of course there had been warning signs, such as Peggy's restlessness, reticence, and increasing tendency to go out without me at night. But I had refused to see the signs and missed a million clues because I wanted to miss them. Peggy said our relationship had become boring and predictable and she needed a change. I liked boring and predictable in a relationship. Perhaps Peggy and I had never been as well-suited to one another as I had thought. "We're stuck in the same old routine,"

Peggy complained. "You'll be happier with something new also. You gotta shake it up from time to time." Peggy claimed she wanted to stay friends, but she left without giving me her new phone number or address. I never saw her again.

Right after Peggy left, I was a wreck, and my behavior made it transparent to the director of Mother Goose that she had unwittingly hosted a lesbian couple in her attic for a year and a half. It had apparently not occurred to her before, but the way I came apart when Peggy left made it crystal clear. She called me into her office and terminated my employment. "A homosexual has no business around children, particularly around abused children. What in the world makes you think you can work with children while living your perverted lifestyle?" I was too distraught to remind her of all the excellent work that Peggy and I had done and to point out that we had not molested any children.

I wish I had defended myself and showed more spine when I was fired, but I didn't have the emotional capacity for such a battle at that moment. The director of Mother Goose and I had made fudge together with the children, sat up until midnight watching old movies and eating popcorn with the teenagers, run around the yard squirting hoses and tossing water balloons at screeching youngsters in the heat of August. We had been friends, co-workers, allies, and colleagues. I was stunned that the instant she discovered I was a lesbian, everything changed and she was convinced I posed a danger to the children. My sexual preference instantly erased over a year of camaraderie.

As I began to pack my things, I called my best friend, Ross, and poured my heart out. I had lost Peggy, my job, my home, and my dear children who lived there. I had lost my self-assurance and my bearings. What I didn't immediately realize was that Ross rejoiced in my losses. He had been waiting for those losses to occur. He had bided his time and he believed that his moment had arrived.

At first, after we split, Ross didn't go out with anyone else. But before long, he took advantage of the separation, which he viewed as temporary, to date other women. He didn't have sex with any of them. Neither one of us was built for casual intimacy. He did, however, enjoy going out with other women and flirting heavily. Some of the women he dated during that time became good friends of his. He never suffered for lack of companionship. His mother's friends at the synagogue and his aunts considered him a highly eligible bachelor. These would-be matchmakers, who could not resist that kind of raw material, embarked on a determined campaign to marry him off. They competed for his time, each one hoping to take credit for introducing him to his final chosen bride. For his part, Ross cultivated the art of the blind date. When home with his parents, he went to the matchmakers' dinner parties and events. He once told me he was trapped in a Jewish Jane Austen novel. It never occurred to me when we separated that he would remain convinced I would go back to him.

The minute he hung up from my desperate phone call, he jumped into his car, certain that I was about to fall far and fast back into his arms. When I met him at the door to my attic room at Mother Goose, he practically glowed, even though he tried to appear somber. I had acquired few possessions during my undergraduate years. Ross helped me pack my belongings into boxes, but I had not arranged to move anywhere with the boxes. Ross was able to fit all my earthly possessions into his Volkswagen van. We loaded it up and drove the length of the tree-shaded driveway of Mother Goose for the last time as I sobbed.

Ross suggested he take me to my parents' house, where I could regroup. I phoned Mama and told her I had lost my job and was suffering from a failed romance, that Ross was with me, and that I wanted to move back home for a while. She attempted to console me. It was late in the day by the time we hung up so Ross and I checked into a roadside dive called the Camelot Motel for the night. A large picture of a ruined castle hung above the bed. The castle looked romantic, picturesque, and melancholy. I tried to imagine how it might have looked when it was built up and I wondered if a picture of it in its heyday hung in a different room of the motel. I soaked for nearly an hour in a hot bath, as if the heat could sweat the pain from my heart.

I emerged from the steamy depths of the bathroom rosy, scented, and wrapped in a white, floor-length robe. I lay on my back on the bed, staring at the ceiling. Ross lay down beside me and stroked my damp hair, massaged my head, and rubbed my shoulders. In my distracted state, at first I didn't realize what was happening but then Ross leaned over and kissed me.

I sat bolt upright.

"I'm sorry," I fumbled. "I didn't, I mean, I don't, I mean, you must still have hopes that you and I, but it's not. Oh no." I tapped my chest with my fingertips. "This is a broken heart, not an identity crisis." Large silent tears rolled down my cheeks. "I'm hopeless. I can't do anything right."

As I spoke, Ross sat back cross-legged on the bed and leaned against the headboard. He folded his hands in his lap and stared down at them.

"Imagine you have a good friend who's a gay guy and he has a crush on you," I tried to explain. "And he begs you to sleep with him. And because you love him, you consider it for a fraction of a second. You think maybe you'll do it just once. But then you come to your senses and realize that you can't get into having sex with a guy, no matter how much you care about him. It's not who you are. I can't do it Ross. I'm a lesbian. Just because Peggy left me doesn't change who I am."

"So what about me? Who am I to you?"

"I thought we resolved that a long time ago," I answered, as the truth about his continuing expectations became obvious. "But I guess not."

"Then why do you call me whenever something big happens in your life? Why do you want me to share all your successes and failures? Why do you expect me to pick up the pieces when you fall apart?"

"Because you're my dearest friend in the whole world. If you love someone very much, you have to love them on their own terms as best you can. Can't you love me as a friend for who I am? Without the romantic relationship?"

"Not with our history, I can't."

"I never meant to mislead you into thinking that there could be anything more than friendship between us." It was not until that moment that Ross finally heard the truth and believed it. He put his face in his hands and wept. I wrapped him in my arms and wept with him. I could not be the woman he wanted me to be.

That night, we held each other and talked about everything. We remembered our teen years together, recalling many of our adventures. He talked about the changes he had gone through after our separation and the women he had dated. I talked about Peggy and Mother Goose. I reinforced for Ross the fact that I would never cross back over the line into heterosexuality, but this was not really necessary as he finally understood that he and I had no future together. Eventually, exhausted, we fell into fitful sleep. We slept late and woke up groggy. Neither one of us was in the mood for breakfast so we skipped it and stopped later on for a quick lunch at a diner.

When we checked out of the Camelot, we closed the door forever on our childhood romance. Ross drove me home and helped me unload at my parents' house. After we emptied the van, Mama offered Ross a bowl of homemade soup, but he declined. I walked him out. Before he got into the van, Ross gripped my wrist with a fierceness that frightened me. "I need time. I don't want to see you for a while. Don't call me," he commanded.

I told my parents there had been a shake-up at Mother Goose and I had lost my job and that I had been seeing someone I could have taken seriously but it ended badly. I said I didn't want to talk about it, and that I needed time to figure out what I wanted to do next. Papa played endless games of cards with me in the evenings and Mama cooked me gourmet dinners and yummy desserts. The teaching credential course at Vassar was still open to me, but I didn't have the heart to return. After a week mooning around the house, I telephoned Rina and asked if I could stay with her in the city for a few days.

Standing on the front stoop of Rina's townhouse in Harlem, I realized that my preoccupation with my own nonsense had distracted me so much that I hadn't even thought to pick up a gift for Rina, whom I hadn't seen in months. I remembered I had a couple of cassette tapes in my bag. I could buy them again for myself and give mine away to Rina.

Through the long, slender panels of beveled glass set in the heavy oak door, I saw Arthur's shape approach. "Hey, little sister," he greeted in his rumbling bass voice. He gave me a warm hug. "Rina," he called into the depths of the house, "Sarah's here."

Arthur led me through the comfortable chaos of their living room to the studio, where Rina, drawing pen in hand, met me in the doorway with a hug and kisses on both cheeks. Rina wore a paint-spattered faded T-shirt and plaid cotton shorts. Her bare feet sported deep purple toenail polish.

"I love the toenail polish," I told her.

"Arthur says it looks like I slammed my foot in the car door," she replied, abandoning her pen on the drawing table and clicking off the high-intensity lamp. "Can I get you anything to eat or drink?"

"A glass of water, please."

We went into the kitchen. The windows stood open and the fragrant scent of geraniums and marigolds drifted in from the back yard. I took a deep breath, as if I hadn't inhaled fresh air in months. I sat across from Rina at the kitchen table while Arthur took a turquoise pitcher out of the refrigerator and poured water into a Mason jar for me.

"You look tired. What's going on with you?" Rina asked.

"Ah, me; my least favorite subject. Do I really look that tired?"

"No, not at all," Arthur said, throwing Rina a reproving glance. "You look terrific."

I took a drink of water from the Mason jar. "Hey, I brought you something." I opened my bag and pulled out the cassette tapes, which I passed across the table. "These are some of my favorites. Have you ever listened to these musicians?"

Rina thanked me as she examined the tapes, reading the names of the songs and the musicians. Then Rina looked up sharply and pinned me in her on-the-mark gaze. "This is women's music. What's the deal, Sarah? Are you into women now?"

I nearly choked on my water. I turned crimson and then I laughed so hard I couldn't talk. The tapes were music written and performed by lesbians, and Rina had taken one look, recognized the musicians, and figured me out, that fast.

"I'm sorry," I gasped. They waited for me to catch my breath and when I finally did, I said,

"I have successfully hidden the truth about myself from so many people for so long because those people didn't want to see the truth. And it took so little for you to figure it out. It's too funny; and a relief, you know, to have someone in the family see me for who I am. I can't tell Mama and Papa. Papa would hit the roof. And Sophie is so conservative."

Arthur sat down next to me and, taking my hand in both of his, demanded sternly in a mock preacher's voice, "Alright, Ms. Sarah, what the heck is going on with you?"

I spilled the beans. I told them about Peggy. I told them about Mother Goose and how much I had loved it there and then about getting fired. And finally I told them about Ross, who, unbeknownst to me, had waited for me for two years until I smashed his heart to bits. It made a big difference to have them know about me. Arthur and Rina made it so easy. They didn't get hung up on the fact that I was a lesbian. That was a non-issue. They went right past that to the real issues, like my broken heart and confusion about what to do next with my life.

"I agree with you that you can't go back to Vassar," Rina said. "Everything there will just remind you of the past and you need to look forward. You need a change."

"What do you suggest?"

"You could teach at a private school for a year or two. You don't need a credential to do that, do you?" Rina asked.

"Could you see me at a Catholic girls' school? I don't think so."

"Why not?" Rina asked. I gave her a stern look. "Alright, well maybe not an all-girls school."

"You could still study for your credential," Arthur pointed out. "You don't have to go to Vassar to do that. Do it somewhere else."

"I like that idea, but I think it's too late to apply anywhere else for the fall semester."

"Maybe not. We have friends in California. I can give them a call and see what might be arranged," Arthur offered.

"California! That would definitely be a change," I said with a dry laugh.

The next morning, Arthur called TJ, who had gone to art school with him and Rina, and who lived in Berkeley. By that afternoon, TJ called back with the names and numbers of people who could provide me with more information about the credentialing program at Cal-Berkeley. I spoke to one of them, who was extraordinarily helpful and sympathetic, and after that things moved quickly. TJ had a friend with clout in the education department; a friend who owed him a favor. He offered to call in the favor on my behalf. I had nothing to lose so I decided to pursue this option.

Although Papa complained bitterly about the distance when I announced I was going to move to Berkeley, he was relieved that I had charted a new course and seemed to be emerging from my funk.

On my last weekend on the East Coast before I departed for California, I accompanied Mama into the city to see a museum exhibit of Chinese arts and crafts. As we strolled through the exhibition, I experienced a growing sense of anxiety. I wondered if I was having a "panic attack," which I had read about in psychology textbooks. After a half an hour of studying cases of women's personal care possessions, such as jade and wooden hair-sticks, hand-mirrors painted with tiny flowers, and combs carved with birds, I was possessed by a surge of fear.

My throat constricted and I could barely breathe.

"Sit here," Mama commanded, putting her arm around me and guiding me toward a bench. Then the strangest thing happened. I physically recoiled from her. I could not bear to have Mama touch me. Her voice, her very proximity, made me feel sick to my stomach. I desperately needed to get out of the exhibition. I reached for the wall to steady myself as I stumbled out of the room and collapsed on a bench near the entrance. I put my head down on my lap. Mama hovered at my elbow and put a hand on my back. I wanted her to take her hand off me. "Maybe we should go outdoors," she suggested.

"No, I'll be OK in a minute," I managed to say as I sat up and shrugged her hand off. "You go back in and enjoy yourself. I'm OK now, really. I'll just sit here for a while and join you later."

"Are you sure?" Mama hesitated, worried.

"Yes. Go."

Mama turned in the arched entranceway to reassure herself that I really wanted her to go. She was framed by two gigantic porcelain vases encased in glass that stood sentry at the yawning mouth of the exhibition. The delicate burnt-orange and black painting of tree branches on the vases threaded out into a confusing map to nowhere. My throat tightened. I couldn't wait for Mama to disappear and I couldn't think of a reasonable explanation for any of it.

After Mama left, I calmed down. I took a novel out of my bag and read. Soon I became drowsy and I leaned back against the wall and closed my eyes. Images drifted into my mind as I floated between sleep and waking. I smelled the scent of flowers, strong as ripe melons. Then I entered a room in which Chinese guards stood at attention. They were clothed in red and gold. It was a humid evening. A slight breeze moved the damp air. There were lush gardens somewhere nearby. I saw a handsome man with a smooth, muscular chest and gentle, work-worn fingers. He had deep eyes that wrinkled at the corners from many years of laughter. The man melted as I startled and woke with a rush of grief. The man's eyes burned in my memory.

When Mama emerged from the exhibit, I felt a surge of anger toward her. Shaken and drained by the mysterious emotions of the day, I just wanted to go home. Mama's concern, which was entirely justified, irritated me. I said little on the walk to the train and once seated I avoided conversation by burying myself in my book. I had the feeling I was looking at something important and not seeing it. The Asian museum pieces. The twilight vision of the man and the gardens. My irrational anger at Mama. I could not make sense of the emotions and images of the day.

The next morning, I moved to California.

I arrived in Berkeley on a bright August afternoon. I took the Airporter from San Francisco International Airport to a downtown hotel, and TJ's roommate Lee (another friend of Rina's) met me there in a beat-up gray Toyota. I had shipped a few belongings on ahead and carried only one suitcase with me. TJ was still at work when I entered my new home for the first time. I remembered TJ as the sort of person who was the life of the party, and I hoped I wouldn't bore him to death with my reclusive tendencies. Lee poured me a glass of lemonade and showed me my room, which I liked instantly. It was large with a high ceiling and a walk-in closet. It overlooked the back yard, which was planted with flowers and tomatoes. There was a bed in it, but no other furniture. Lee explained that the landlord stored furniture in the basement and told me to go down there to look when I was ready to choose a dresser, desk, bookshelf, or anything else I wanted. I opened the window, sprawled across the bed, and promptly fell asleep.

TJ's booming voice woke me up. "Where's our little sister?" he called to Lee as he rolled into the living room in his wheelchair. A few moments later I heard a gentle tap at my door.

"Come in," I said.

"Welcome!" TJ greeted me exuberantly. "Are you ready to choose some furniture?"

"I kind of like it this way. Spare."

"No, really. I brought a couple of muscle-bound friends home with me to help carry the stuff up from the basement. Go see what's down there," TJ urged.

So I went downstairs and chose a dresser, a desk and chair, a nightstand, a bookshelf, a long narrow mirror with etched decor around the edges, a big overstuffed chair, a standing lamp, and a spindly coat rack. TJ's friends helped me arrange the furniture in my room, then they retired to the living room to listen to music. As I unpacked, I felt at home for the first time since leaving Mother Goose.

When my classes began, I became completely absorbed in school. I could have made time for a rich social life, but I didn't want one. At first Lee and TJ tried to include me in everything they did; but, as I repeatedly declined their invitations, they soon realized I preferred a more solitary lifestyle. So they went about their busy social lives while I remained ensconced in my cozy room. I wrote in my journal, sketched, and painted in watercolors. I attended classes and lectures at the Zen Center. I went above and beyond for my courses in the credentialing program. I had a particular interest in learning more about classroom management philosophies and techniques that sought to empower rather than control children. This seemed to be a new approach and there was not much literature out there about it.

In the spring I began my student teaching assignment, which turned out to be completely different from anything I had anticipated. I worked under the eagle-eye of the teacher to whom I had been assigned. After thirty years in the classroom, she had rigid, old-fashioned ideas about teaching. Getting along with Mrs. Polschak required all the restraint I could muster. She was a strict disciplinarian, who actually made children stand in the corner when she was unhappy with their behavior. She had no tolerance for the noise and chaos of children that I believed necessary for real learning. My greatest challenge in working with her was that I felt that children deserved the same respect given to adults whereas Mrs. Polschak viewed children as untamed animals requiring a firm hand.

In the end, I resigned myself to making it through the student teaching in one piece to obtain my credential. Next year, I told myself, when I have my own classroom and I can work with my students from the day they cross my threshold, then I will establish my own ground rules and do a better job of teaching.

Living with TJ and Lee provided me with automatic friends, so I didn't feel the need to look much further than my home for companionship. Although TJ socialized a great deal, he also had a quiet side and he invested time in getting to know me. He would often poke his head into my room in the evening to see if I wanted to talk with him. He was interested in my ideas about teaching and we had good conversations about my studies and my philosophy of education. It was comforting to know that I could rely on TJ in a pinch. I got along with Lee as a roommate, but she had too many things going on in her life to spend much time at home with me or TJ.

My one indulgence (and I had to laugh at myself for even considering it an indulgence) was walking by the bay or the ocean. I frequently went to the Berkeley Marina in the evening to watch the sun descend in a huge orange ball into the rhythmic motion of the water. Watching the sunset over the water reminded me of our family's summer vacations at the Jersey Shore when my sisters and I were children.

One evening, while sharing a spaghetti dinner we had made, TJ asked me, "Don't you want to meet someone? You know, like a relationship partner sort of someone?"

"Eventually."

"You have to go out to do that, you know. It's not likely that you'll meet someone in our driveway."

"I don't have the energy for it right now. I have other things on my mind. Honestly, I'm partnered-out at the moment."

"That bad?"

I flashed him my most enigmatic Mona-Lisa smile. "Let's just say my excursions into relationships have been discouraging and exhausting and leave it at that. I'm directing my attention elsewhere these days."

Despite my efforts to not dwell on the past, I couldn't shake the pain of losing Peggy. Sometimes in my bed at night, I longed for Peggy's touch with an unbearable hunger. In my mind's eye I could see Peggy's vivid green eyes, the way she tossed her hair, and the curve of her wrist. I remembered the sound of her laughter with startling clarity. I could not forget my desire for her and our love-making that had transported me. I ached for a woman to lie next to me at night, to curl into the nest of each other's arms, where we could leave the cares of the world outside the circle of our embrace. Yet

I could not bring myself to make any effort to meet someone.

In the spring I graduated from my credentialing program. Papa refused to set foot on an airplane so Mama came by herself for my graduation ceremony. We went sight-seeing in San Francisco, hitting all the tourist spots, such as the Golden Gate Bridge, Chinatown, and Fisherman's Wharf. We spent a day in Golden Gate Park where we visited the Steinhart Aquarium, the Academy of Sciences, the Japanese Tea Garden, and the De Young Museum. We took the ferry to Sausalito one evening for dinner. I returned to the East Coast with Mama to visit with the family.

Bearing photographs of TJ and Lee and our house and yard in Berkeley, I took the train into the city to see Rina and Arthur. They were expecting a baby and were in the process of reorganizing and repainting a room in preparation for the baby's arrival. Rina had not informed our parents about the baby herself. Instead, Sophie, who was expecting her second child, had broken the news to them.

While I was visiting, Sophie wanted to talk about the rift in our family ad nauseam. I tried to stay as disengaged from the feud as possible and I advised Sophie to do the same. She claimed she couldn't stay disengaged and that she was stuck in the middle. I felt grateful that I lived on the other side of the country, far away from all that family drama. I wondered how I would keep a long-term relationship secret from my parents and Sophie if I ever did have the good fortune to meet someone in the distant future.

Upon my return to Berkeley, I began to apply for teaching jobs for the fall. To tide me over, I picked up a summer job as a camp counselor. I refereed capture-the-flag and kickball, gave swimming lessons, and supervised messy outdoor art projects. The job was easy and fun. By the time the summer ended, I had landed a position teaching a second/third-grade split class. On the day that I received the call from the principal offering me the job, TJ and Lee took me out to eat to celebrate.

In August I attended a weeklong orientation training provided by the school district. A few days before school started, I was assigned to my classroom and I went in to set up. I would be teaching what they called a "Challenge Class," administrative code words for children with "behavior problems." Capturing and holding the attention of these children would require every ounce of ingenuity and imagination I could muster. I thought about Peggy and the things Peggy did that inspired children to love her and respond to her.

On the first day of school I studied with mounting excitement the freshly scrubbed faces of my students as they arrived. I could not wait to get to know these children. I greeted them as they entered and showed them where to put their things in cubbies that I had decorated for them. My plan was to give them a tour of the classroom, to explain the different work areas, and to share with them some of the topics I wanted to explore with them during the year. But I discovered instantly that my plan was too ambitious. My first task would be to get their attention.

Three boys chased each other around the classroom. One girl hid in her cubby and sucked her thumb. She would need to be coaxed out, but I was busy dealing with two other girls who were hitting each other with books. While I attempted to separate them, a large boy with curly hair attached himself to my leg and would not let go, causing me to lose all credibility with the book-beating girls. Meanwhile, a group of children had found the stapler on my desk and they were folding paper airplanes and stapling them together as fast as their little hands could move. The paper airplanes swooping through the air made a bigger dent in my self-confidence than anything else since my mental image of an out-of-control classroom was one in which children were throwing paper airplanes. These children had been under my supervision for all of fifteen minutes and my classroom was in utter chaos.

It was at that juncture that the principal popped his head in the door. I was mortified. He took in the scene and immediately clapped his hands, which elicited silence, and then he announced sternly that anyone who didn't sit in his or her seat within the next ten seconds would be accompanying him to the front office. The children stared at him blankly while one bold boy piped up, "We don't know where our seats are."

The principal turned to me, a vein in his neck bulging. "I suggest you assign these children to seats as quickly as possible," he instructed curtly.

I rushed over to my desk and picked up a stack of colorful name tags that I had made the previous day. "If you children would choose a seat, we can put your name on your desk for you," I announced. The principal looked at me disdainfully and said nothing while the children reluctantly shuffled over to select their desks. Two boys started to argue over a seat. "Pete," the principal cautioned one of them threateningly. Pete moved to a different seat, muttering under his breath. The principal turned to me and said, loudly, so that everyone could hear, "If Pete gives you any trouble, just send him to me. We're old friends." The fact that he would say this publicly seemed rude to me. I could only imagine how Pete must have felt when he heard this comment.

"Ladies and gentlemen, don't make me come back down here," the principal warned the children. "You listen to your teacher and do what she tells you. I promise you that anyone who misbehaves will spend the rest of the day in my office." He turned to me. "If anyone in here gives you any trouble, you send them directly to me." He stalked out of the room before I could formulate a reply.

I realized with dismay that I was not going to be able to lecture these children for even a minute because they wouldn't sit still for that long. They had the collective attention span of a pack of terriers set loose in a bird sanctuary. I would have to begin an activity immediately. I distributed paper and crayons and instructed them to draw sea creatures while I moved among them commenting on their progress, keeping them on task, and asking them questions about their work.

Then I formed them into groups of five and gave each group a large piece of butcher paper. Their next assignment was to combine the pictures made by the members of their group by pasting them onto the butcher paper and then to add to the "scene" by drawing on the butcher paper. They were to make an "ocean" with all the sea creatures created by their group. These activities went fairly smoothly with not too many disagreements occurring and, with carefully focused effort, I was able to handle the situations that arose. I was determined to use conflicts as teachable moments and not merely occasions for discipline.

By lunch time, I desperately needed a break from the children. I lined my class up and took them to the cafeteria. As I was walking back to my classroom, a woman with long, blond hair intercepted me. The woman held out her hand to shake mine as she introduced herself. "I'm Marjorie, pleased to meet you," she said. I shook her hand and told her my name was Sarah. She continued, "So you got the two/three Challenge Class this year?"

"That's what they call it."

"I've been teaching here for years. If you need to talk to someone, I'm in room six. The boss created the Challenge Classes," she informed me as she gestured her head in the direction of the administrative offices. "What a disaster."

I kept my face neutral. I had the impression that Marjorie was a chatterbox, so I was pretty sure she would explain what she meant if I didn't cut her off. I was right. She chattered on. "He puts all the extremely emotionally needy children, all the children with real problems, into one class, to keep them out of the other classes. It makes it even harder for them to learn and it makes it impossible to teach them. He does it because of the way the state tracks the success of the school, by classroom achievement. He also does it because it's easier to teach the other children if the most disruptive ones are removed. His method keeps his school track record for achievement high, which makes him look good. Usually he gives the Challenge Classes to the teachers he doesn't like. When he runs out of disfavored teachers, he gives them to the new teachers. You got a bad break. If there's anything I can do to help, just holler."

I thanked Marjorie for the information and excused myself so I could eat my lunch in solitude and mull over her words. The "challenge" of the Challenge Class, it seemed, was going to be more mine than the children's.

I was determined to use a positive approach to maintaining order in my classroom, and I was equally determined to teach my students the content they needed to master at their grade level. I decided I would have to find a way to provide as much one-on-one time with each child as possible. I would set up a lot of small group activities, train the children to work together cooperatively so they could learn from one another, and then circulate so I could interact with individual children. In my mind, I threw out the lesson plans I had prepared for the first three months. I would get to know each and every one of them as quickly as I could. Each of these children needed an individualized learning plan. I knew what had to be done, the question was, could I do it? Could only one person physically do it?

After lunch, the children went outside for P.E. and they came back to me more subdued. We listed words on the blackboard that described their sea creatures. I wrote the words. They copied them on a piece of lined paper. One boy, desperate for my attention, ate the paper I gave him for his list. A few minutes before the end of the day, the curly-headed boy once again wrapped himself around my leg and wouldn't let go. Two children got into a fist-fight and then chased each other around the classroom. I couldn't move to intervene because of the boy on my leg. The class slipped into the same pandemonium with which the day had started, but, mercifully, the bell rang and the children ran screaming out of my room, which they left in a disastrous state.

I stood in the doorway and watched the children race across the school yard to the waiting buses. Then I heard sniffles and sobs, which I tracked to their source, and discovered a child on the floor under a table crying. I picked him up and dried his tears with a tissue. "What happened?" I asked.

"Chucky punched me and knocked me down," he whined.

"We'll talk to Chucky about that first thing tomorrow," I informed him grimly. "Now you better hurry or you'll miss your bus."

I cleaned the classroom and set up for the next day. Then I took a deep breath and marched determinedly to the principal's office. He looked up in surprise as I entered and closed the door behind myself.

"What can I do for you?" he asked, casting his gaze up and down my body.

"I need an aide in my classroom," I announced, struggling to conceal my irritation caused by the "once-over" male scrutiny with which he had just bombarded my body.

He slid his glasses down his nose and peered at me over the top of them condescendingly. "So you're having difficulty handling your class?"

I knew it was not a question. He was attempting to demoralize me and I was not buying it. "Anyone would have difficulty handling that class. And you know exactly why. The distribution of emotionally needy students for this peer group is weighted heavily into my classroom."

He said nothing.

"Since you have made the choice to isolate the difficult students from the rest of the population, you will have to make some provision for at least attempting to teach these youngsters."

"I don't have to do anything," he replied imperiously.

"You have to provide public education," I snapped. "It's the law." We glared at each other. "I need an aide to facilitate more one-on-one for these youngsters. In fact, I need about fifteen aides, but one will have to suffice." What was the worst he could do? Fire me? So what?

"We only provide aides to assist with severely disabled children," he responded. "That's the standard policy."

"I will spare you my opinion about your standard policy. Listen, you clearly don't want to deal with the children in my classroom. I am willing to deal with them for you, but I need some support here. I want an aide. Immediately."

"You're a feisty one aren't you? I like that."

He seemed to think he had put me in the proper box and figured out how to handle me. And he most certainly believed I needed to be "handled." He was getting a kick out of me in that male you're-so-cute-when-you're-angry sort of way, and it required all the self-control I could muster to refrain from hurling insults at him, not to mention a stapler or his coffee cup.

"I'll arrange for you to have an aide in your class by the end of the week," he promised with a paternalistic smile.

"Thank you." I turned on my heel and exited before he could do something over-the-top infuriating, like patting me on the behind.

That evening I walked in the front door of our house and got as far as the sofa before my legs collapsed. I fell asleep for an hour until Lee came in.

"Rough first day?" Lee asked.

"Challenging."

After my nap, I reworked my lesson plans for the rest of the week. I would teach these children how to have an attention span. I would teach them how to learn. I planned to go back to the fundamentals from kindergarten, like socialization skills and good citizenship skills. I was determined to earn their trust and their affection so they would be intrinsically motivated to please me and to take pride in their accomplishments. The academic curriculum would have to wait while I trained these children to be teachable. I did not want to become one of those teachers who "manages" the students. I wanted to discover who the children were and bring out the best in them rather than imposing something on them from the outside. I wanted to draw something out of them from their inside.

To his credit, the principal did provide me with an aide by the end of the week. My aide, Ginny, was my first and most important stroke of luck. I called her "The Rock" because of her unflappability. Ginny was intuitive and could take my glance or gesture for its exact meaning and noiselessly follow my most subtle direction. I used Ginny to provide one-on-one time to children, directing her throughout the day to activities with individual children, spreading her around, allowing her to develop personal relationships with all the children, but especially with the ones who had the highest emotional need. This had a remarkably calming effect on the class.

I reached out to the children's parents and invited them into the classroom. The result was that I usually had at least one parent helping at any given time, and very often more than one. I allowed parents to bring babies and younger siblings into the class when they came to help. My classroom had a family atmosphere. Ginny and I modeled for parents how to seize teachable moments, how to relate respectfully to children, and how to inspire children to do the right thing because they wanted to and not because they would be punished or rewarded for their actions.

Ginny's most impressive credentials, in my opinion, were that she had raised four children of her own and she had two grandchildren.

"You should write a book about teaching," Ginny kept telling me. But I didn't need to write a book. There were other educators, who thought along the same lines as I, who had already written books. I had read them. I was not particularly original. That first year that I spent in the classroom, I was too busy developing my curriculum to do any further research or reading about cutting-edge practices in education.

Some of my lesson plans worked and others crashed and burned. On some days, Ginny and I wept together in exhaustion and discouragement after the children had gone home. On other days, we counted small successes, and on the occasional really good days we celebrated. One way or another, we made it through the year; and when I stood at the end of it, and surveyed the terrain I had covered, I marveled at how much I had learned.

In June, I put in a request to have Ginny as my aide again the following year. I enrolled in a couple of post-graduate classes at Stanford for the summer and bought a little Volkswagen for the commute. If Lee and TJ thought they would see more of me when the school year ended, they thought wrong. I buried myself in my studies, preparing for my next year of teaching.

I taught that Challenge Class for three years with Ginny by my side and then I resigned. That idiot principal had started to use my class as an example of how well his system for segregating the children with "behavior problems" worked. I wanted no part of it. My children needed to be included in the other classrooms, not lumped together and removed to their own island like lepers.

I took a job at a private school for gifted children, where I faced a whole different set of challenges. Meanwhile I had entered a degree program in school administration that accommodated working teachers. I took my classes at night, on weekends, and over the summer. I moved out of TJ and Lee's house and rented my own apartment not far from them.

During my years in Berkeley, I conscientiously avoided any relationship that might have romantic overtones, refusing to go out on dates and instead spending time with tried-and-true friends, most often Ginny and her husband Herb and their family. I could not seem to stop or change that discouraging "tape" that kept playing in my head, telling me that I had failed at having a relationship with a man and failed at having a relationship with a woman and I was hopeless at relationships. I figured Peggy had hurt me as my karma for hurting Ross. I threw my love into my students and they gave me enough love in return to satisfy me. As far as romance went, I closed the gates and pulled up the drawbridge to my heart. Occasionally I met someone who would make motions toward swimming the moat and knocking at the door, but I meticulously sent out the crocodiles. The thought of letting someone back in filled me with dread.

On my frequent walks by the water, I watched couples as they meandered hand-in-hand on beaches, piers, and paths. Sometimes I saw lesbian couples and they made me feel jealous and wistful. I wondered how they maintained healthy relationships.

After I completed my master's degree in school administration, I took a break from teaching in order to return to school full-time to earn a doctorate in education. Papa kept a bulletin board in his den where he posted newspaper clippings that I sent him about my activities, such as the announcement for a series of parenting classes I taught at the public library, an article about the success of my Challenge Class, and, at last, the local paper's notice of my graduation from Stanford with my doctorate.

The most exciting aspect of my studies at Stanford was that I connected with other educators who shared my beliefs about the way children should be treated and how to develop the full potential of youngsters. I was at the forefront of work with cooperative learning, parent involvement in the schools, and what was referred to as "character education." I studied and practiced with other educators who believed in child-centered education and child-centered classrooms. New research confirmed ideas that I had long held true but couldn't previously prove with hard evidence. I could finally justify many of the choices I had made with the children in my Challenge Class.

While attending Stanford, I called Ginny frequently to share a study or report I came across in my research. I read material to her over the phone and Ginny would cluck her tongue and say, "Obviously, ask any grandma and they'll tell you that's the case."

After I completed my doctorate, I decided to return to the East to be closer to the family. My sisters had children and I didn't want to miss out on watching them grow up. I doubted I would ever have any children of my own, so my sisters' children were about as close as I would get. I wanted to be nearby so I could be a part of their daily lives. Also, my parents were getting older and I wanted to spend more time with them before their health began to fail. Truthfully, I never put down deep roots in California.

During my California years, I heard nothing from Ross. Occasionally I asked Mama about him. She told me when he had gotten married and then, a couple of years later, when he and his wife had a baby. One evening during my last few weeks in California, my phone rang and it was Ross. He had chatted with Papa at synagogue and heard I was moving back. He invited me to visit him and his family. It was lovely to hear his voice after so many years of silence. After I hung up the phone, I decided to go for a walk.

I grabbed a sweater and drove up to Point Richmond. The spring air carried the flowery scent of new beginnings. Lovers wandered in pairs on the paths. I walked slowly along the water's edge. California has been good to me. Gold rush country. I found my gold. I would return home triumphant, as an accomplished educator. I turned my back to the wind and looked in the opposite direction from the brilliant sunset. In the tall grass near the road stood a lone egret, balanced on one spindly leg. It looked like a dash of pure white paint against a reedy, green-grey backdrop. Its beak was sharp and accurate, the angles well-defined. With clear intention, the egret surveyed his domain for potential dinner. His beauty took my breath away. What was it that made me stand transfixed, watching, until the exquisite creature purposefully spread his prehistorically shaped wings, and languidly took to the air?

On my last night in California, I slept at Ginny's house. She would drive me to the airport in the morning. Ginny and Herb loved to cook together and they prepared a delicious, all-American meal of fried chicken and biscuits for me, complete with apple pie for dessert. Then we retired to the living room where Herb had his after-dinner brandy and Ginny and I drank tea.

I curled up in a large comfy chair, my feet wrapped under me, like a cat.

"That pie was heavenly," I applauded Herb's mastery in the kitchen.

"You know," Herb reminisced, leaning back on the couch, "I remember once when I was onboard a ship in the navy. I was eating blueberry pie, minding my own business, when something rubbery that I couldn't chew got hung up in my mouth. I pulled it out and opened it flat and would you believe it was the recipe for the pie? We sure teased our cooks about that one!" Herb boomed in his jovial way. Ginny put her arm across the back of the couch and patted Herb on the shoulder. I figured she had probably heard the recipe-in-the-pie story about a million times.

"I admire you two. You've been married for such a long time. How do you make it work?"

Ginny smiled shyly and deferred to Herb, "Why don't you field that one, sweetie."

With a bemused glance at Ginny, Herb answered, "We just keep laughing together."

"I know it's not that simple. I'm sure you've had your moments, like any couple, but you get past them," I said, pressing them to give me a more complete answer.

Ginny could see I was serious and she said, "I think it works because we're both in it for the long haul, always have been. We just know we have to find a way to work things out because we don't give ourselves another choice. It's kind of like you and that Challenge Class that first year; quitting was not an option."

Herb added, "Ginny has never held me back. She has adapted to the ways in which I have changed over the years. And I hope," he patted Ginny on the knee and looked to her for affirmation, "I have always adjusted to her changes too."

"I read somewhere that the reason why insects are the most resilient, persistent, and long-lived species on the planet is because of their adaptability. I guess there's a lesson there for us humans," I told them.

Ginny leaned forward and said confidentially, "Sarah, forgive me for saying so, but you need a husband."

I blushed and nervously twisted the strings on my hoodie.

"You do, dear. You're the kind of homey person who should be married. You won't be happy on your own forever. I know it's none of my business. Well, maybe it is, because I'm a friend who wants the best for you. I just wish that you would entertain the possibility of opening your heart to whatever comes your way when you move back East. Give it a chance. I don't mean to put you on the spot, but I have to say it."

"It isn't that easy for me."

"Anyone with two eyes can see that something happened to you that made you shut down. 'Once burned, twice shy,' they say. But whatever happened is over and done. It's time to move on, sweetie."

"Forgive her," Herb interjected. "You know she can't help it. She worries about you as much as she does about any of our own."

"It's OK."

"Promise me," Ginny insisted, "promise me you will entertain the possibility."

And I thought, OK, I'm ready to do it, so I made that promise to Ginny.

Later that night, before falling asleep, I remembered my jumbled state of mind when I fled to California, a lifetime ago it seemed. I had figured out who I was and come into my own in California. I had constructed a comfortable, fruitful life, independent from any romantic attachment. But Ginny's words touched a nerve. I needed to take a risk, to attempt a relationship. And when the right person came along, I would try to build a partnership, not deliberately, like a fact, but intuitively, like an organic process. I would open my heart to possibility, pain, joy, all of it. I would open my heart to love.